Stefanie Dawn

Demonic
Novella

Stefanie Dawn

This book is a work of fiction. Any references to real events, real people, and real places are used fictitiously. Other names, characters, places and incidents are products of the Author's imagination and any resemblance to persons, living or dead, actual events, organizations or places is entirely coincidental.

All rights are reserved. This book is intended for the purchaser of this book ONLY. No part of this book may be reproduced or transmitted in any form or by any means, graphic, electronic, or mechanical, including photocopying, recording, taping, or by any information storage retrieval system, without the express written permission of the Author. All songs, song titles and lyrics contained in this book are the property of the respective songwriters and copyright holders.

Disclaimer: The material in this book contains graphic language and sexual content and is intended for mature audiences, ages 18 and older.

ISBN: 978-1763870475

Editing and Proofing by Swish Design & Editing
Book Design by Swish Design & Editing
Cover Design by Patrisha Badalo of
Art Muse Graphic Designs
Published by Angels and Fire Books
Cover Image Copyright 2023

First Edition

DEDICATION

Who do you even dedicate a smutty book
about a demon to?

DEMONIO

CHAPTER

1

My hands ached under his grip, a grip which didn't waiver despite the sweat dripping from my wrists under his palms—skin on skin, in the most primal way. The demon had me pinned in my kitchen, in a house that was no longer my home. I ached for him in a way I'd never experienced before, and despite him being a supernatural force I could neither contain nor understand, all I could think of was shredding my clothes from my body and pressing against his. He was already naked, having arrived in my home like that, just as God had made him.

Or the Devil.

My shirt stuck to my chest under the heat radiating from him. The demon's skin was warm, like leaning against a brick wall on a summer's day. A slight touch not registering the burn, but the prolonged contact of his hand holding both of mine sent conflicting sensations through my body as I was torn between wanting to pull away and leaning against his hard body.

You shouldn't mess with powers you don't understand.

The sound of his words still echoed inside my mind, and I tried to ignore his wandering gaze as he restrained me, my arms stretched above my head and the knob from a kitchen drawer pressing painfully into my lower back. But I welcomed the discomfort and focused on the pain, taking anything I could to distract from the warmth that flushed between my legs at his mere proximity and the ache of my clit when I wished his fingers were there instead of holding me still.

How was I supposed to know I would summon an actual demon?

I was just messing around.

Were you?

I couldn't even tell if the voice in my head was mine or his. Was he in my mind? Or was there a part of me clawing from the depths of my consciousness, determined to make me admit the truth?

I *wanted* him to come to me.

Desperately.

I called to him from across the realms of Earth and Hell. I told myself it wouldn't work, that summonings weren't real, giving myself all sorts of excuses for why I did what I did. But with a fever that burned inside my mind, I wanted so much for it to be real. Apparently, I wanted it enough for it to happen. Because I'd been broken down into a shadow of my former self, and now I was faced with that, I realized my previous self wasn't much of a person to break down. I was nothing more than the pieces other people decided I should be made of, thrown together and held there by the cage of the life I'd accepted as mine.

So, here was what I asked for—a being to free me and seek the revenge I couldn't, naked and restraining me as I ached for his touch. I could barely comprehend the words he was saying as his hardness pressed against my stomach. Distracting me every time I shifted, I told myself I was trying to get away, knowing I wanted to be closer.

"What do you want from me?" I managed to meet his eyes, glowing with a fire burning behind dark and dilated pupils.

"You summoned me. You offered me your soul in exchange for revenge."

My mouth was dry, and I tried to swallow,

clinging to the discomfort of the action when all I wanted to do was moan and grind against him as he pressed his hips harder against mine. His lip twitched, lifting into a barely-there smirk as he thrust his hips forward, his length pressed against my stomach.

Was this a trick?

A lure of an evil power that had me willing to surrender myself to him?

"My soul?" I choked out the words. "So after I die, I go to Hell?"

He chuckled, and I bit my lip against the whimper rising in my throat. The lack of friction against my aching clit was agonizing, and the throbbing of blood through my body was the loudest sound in the room, distracting me from the increasingly small part of myself that reminded me I was in a serious situation.

Concentrate on what he's saying.

But from the moment he had appeared in my house, I'd been able to think of nothing else but submitting to him.

Of *fucking* him.

Because *sex* didn't seem like enough.

The word didn't encompass what I wanted him to do to me, and *making love* was a far cry from the images in my mind. I don't think I've ever said *fuck* out loud in my life, but now the words *fuck me* and *please* were pressed insistently against the back of my teeth, crying to be free so he could make my desires a reality.

He was a demon, a temptation sent by the Devil into my home. A temptation I truly struggled to resist. I felt I'd pay any price he asked if he would only touch me in the way I imagined in the filthy images in my mind, his body leaning over mine, claiming me in ways I couldn't possibly put into words.

Next to him, I was purely and laughably naïve.

I was in…

… way over my head.

He smiled, studying me under his brow. "You think your soul is simply something you sacrifice after you die? Something you don't have to think about between now and the moment you leave this mortal realm? No." I shuddered under the intensity of his gaze. Squirming my hands against his hold, the demon's eyes flickered to the movement as I flexed my fingers. "You'll devote your life to me. You'll worship me. In turn, I'll worship you and your body in any way I desire. From now until the darkness of eternity swallows us whole, in this realm and the next. You'll be mine."

I tried to swallow again, my heart thumping in a panicked rhythm. "But—"

"So you have to ask yourself, my dear Amelia…" Fire blazed in his eyes, and I froze, feeling as though I was looking into the very pits of Hell through the portal in his pupils. A clawed hand brushed purposely over my breast before it rested on my cheek as the demon held my gaze. "How badly do you want this revenge?"

CHAPTER 2

AMELIA

Three Weeks Earlier

My cell sat in my trembling hands, one notification after another appearing, scrolling past my eyes in a wave of horror that never seemed to end and made my heart ache and split open. Did I even know this many people? Some of the numbers weren't even saved in my cell—strangers telling me they hated me for what I had done.

For something I *hadn't done.*

I couldn't *breathe* and clutched at my chest as I watched my life fall apart on the small screen in front of me, blinking every time the tears blurred the words. Everyone I knew was turning against me. The walls of the cozy life I had built with my husband were crumbling, stripping me of everything I held dear and thought made me who I was. Every new person who came in with their abuse shredded away another part of me and left me wondering not only who I was now but who I had been before.

Before. Because now, my life would be divided into two very clear fractions—*before* and *after* the day my life fell apart, and my life was taken from me.

How could Owen *do* this to me?

The photos. Those intimate photographs I hadn't been keen on taking in the first place were not only all over the internet but had been sent to everyone I knew. My husband's face wasn't in any of them. No, he'd made sure to crop that part out. Only I was visible in compromising positions with an expression of wanton ecstasy on my face as I was penetrated from behind. The man in the photographs could be anybody, and as far as everyone knew, he was some random person I had picked up to have sex with.

I choked back a sob.

Owen was the first and only person I'd ever slept with, but the truth didn't seem to matter anymore.

The notifications on my cell kept coming.

Whore.
Slut.
Don't ever come near my family or me again.
What the fuck is wrong with you?
How can you even show your face in church?

Church. The thought struck me with a stab in the chest, and I heaved another sob.

I'll never be able to go back.

I was a pariah.

The tears came then, too many to blink away, hot and fast down my cheeks, burning with humiliation and fear. I didn't understand why Owen would do this. What had I done to deserve my life being pulled apart? If he didn't want to be married to me anymore, he only had to talk to me. I wouldn't have been happy—I loved him with every ounce of my being—but I would have let him go if that's what he wanted.

It would have hurt, but it would've been better than *this.*

It wasn't enough he cheated on me, but he had to

drag me through the mud too.

And the texts kept coming…

Owen deserves better than you, whore.
No wonder he cheated on you.

Owen had told everyone I cheated first and used our intimate pictures as *proof.* Even my family was against me. They loved Owen from the moment we'd met when I was working to save for college and he was in his second year. He came into the diner where I was waitressing, and I think I fell for him on the spot—all messy dark hair and charming smiles.

Did he ever love me? I didn't even know anymore.

He was respectable, from a good family, and was now a doctor.

And the story going around was I'd thrown that picture-perfect life away when *I'd* decided to cheat on *him.* I would *never,* and even the thought of cheating raised bile in my throat. But now, I almost wished I had because the stories hurt so much more when compiled entirely of lies.

Fifteen years of marriage down the drain.

I had no allies.

Nothing left to cling to.

Glancing at my phone as it buzzed again, a screenshot of my image from a public porn site sprang onto my screen with a text from a woman I would've previously called my best friend.

Is this you? LOL. I'm glad you got caught out, cheater. Who can blame Owen for doing the same after you treated him like this?

Lord, please help me through this.

I dropped the phone on the dining table, clasped my hands under my chin, and closed my eyes. My lip trembled as I muttered through a prayer, unable to finish it without another sob raking through my throat. Was this because I didn't want to start a family yet? I wanted a career too. I thought Owen understood that. When I could finally put myself through college, I graduated with a business degree, majoring in marketing. After another two years of hard work, I scored myself a position with the town's largest advertising firm. It wasn't the big-city job I'd dreamed of, but I'd made a life here with Owen. I *loved* my job.

But how could I ever show my face there again?

Owen was in every aspect of my life. All our friends were mutual. Everyone at work knew and loved him. My family loved him, and sometimes, I suspected more than they loved me.

I was alone.

God, please grant me strength.

Dropping my arms, I rested my forehead against the table and cried until I had nothing left to give.

The doorbell woke me, and I lifted my head groggily.

I didn't remember falling asleep. But glancing at the clock on the wall, I realized I must've cried myself to sleep out of sheer exhaustion.

Eight o'clock.

I'd been out for hours.

The doorbell rang again, and I frowned. Surely everyone in the town knew what I was dealing with by now, so who would come to bother me? Were they here to rub it in my face? I didn't think I had a friend left in the world, especially not someone who would take the time to come and see me. Not for anything positive, anyway.

The doorbell rang again, and I sighed.

Pushing myself to my feet, I walked the short hall to the door, eyeing the silhouette through the frosted glass suspiciously. Recognizing it as I reached the foyer, I paused with my hand poised over the handle.

"I know you're in there, Amelia. Open the door."

Anger swelled in my gut, and the words burst from me before I could stop them. "Why should I, Owen? After what you did to me!"

There was a pause, and I dared to think he might actually be feeling guilty. "I rang the doorbell merely as a formality. I still have keys, you know. This is my house too."

When I hesitated, the jingle of keys sounded, the doorknob turned, and I wrenched the door open, determined to take back the small show of power to *let* him in rather than have him push his way forward. When I raised my eyes, I took a stumbling step back at the sight of him. Owen was actually *smiling* at me like this was a social visit and he hadn't just torn my life apart.

Owen was handsome, all his features telling me he was still the person I had trapped in my memories. I hated I could still see the man I fell in love with, and perhaps *still* loved, in his face. I wanted his features to be contorted. I wanted the knowledge of what he was capable of to make him ugly to me. But instead, he was still the man I loved, and all the angry energy simply drained from me as my shoulders slumped, unable to sustain the burst of anger that had come forth only moments before. My love had been thrown away and ground under his boot. The viciousness of the act glinted in his eyes.

I had *nothing* left to give.

He was here, spine straight and eyes clear, as though it was merely another day.

I was *nothing* to him.

"What do you want?" There was barely any volume to my voice. Suddenly exhausted, I simply didn't have the energy to deal with this. Not today. Not tomorrow. Maybe I never would. All I wanted to do was curl up in bed and stay there for days and days and hope that when I came out, all this was over or a bad dream.

Owen thrust an envelope at me as he strolled into our home—*my home.* "Just here to gather some things. We can sort out the house during the divorce proceedings."

"Di-divorce?"

He spun on his heel to face me, giving me another award-winning smile. "Of course, surely you figured that one out?"

I dropped the envelope where I stood, not even

looking at it. Of course, I knew he was divorcing me. That wasn't the part I didn't understand. "Why, Owen? Why did you spread those lies? And those *photos?* They were *private.*" Anguish dripped through me and spilled into my words, but Owen still smiled, and what remained of my heart shattered into dust.

I had to know *why.*

If I could only make sense of this, maybe I wouldn't feel like I was an empty shell of who I was last week. Even who I was yesterday—a woman grappling with the knowledge her husband was leaving for another woman, ten years younger, an administrator from the hospital he worked at.

I would take that over having everything stripped away.

I'd give anything to have yesterday back.

Yesterday, I only lost my husband.

Today, I lost everything.

Owen stepped toward me and reached up, brushing his thumb across my cheek. It took me a second too long to pull away, and I bit my lip, wishing for the pain of my teeth on flesh to help fight the rising tears.

"I have a reputation to maintain, sweetie... you know that." His voice was sugar-sweet, and it sounded so *fake.* Had he always spoken to me like that? I couldn't remember. Everything before today was a haze, a play on a stage he'd built, one he could tear down whenever he wanted to recast his life, starting with me. "I couldn't have the hospital staff thinking I was a cheater and Alison was a homewrecker. How would that look?"

"But what about *my* reputation?" I slapped a palm to my chest, ignoring the tears as they fell. I couldn't stop them, and there was no point in trying. "What about *my* life? *My* job? Don't you care about any of that?"

He simply smiled at me. "Of course I do."

I stood there gaping at him. What could I even say? He didn't care about me, actions spoke louder than words, and he very clearly didn't love me.

"Was any of it real?" I whispered.

When he reached to touch my face again, I slapped his hand away, thankful for at least that show of strength when I thought I had none left. I didn't like confrontation. I was quiet and agreeable. I was one woman at work to get the job done and another at home, and I didn't know how to merge the two to make myself stronger. My achievements at work were more the result of perseverance and keeping clients happy than forcing my way to the top through acts of strength.

How had Owen molded and shaped me into such a pushover?

Or was I always like that?

I couldn't remember, and it didn't matter anymore. Everything from now on would be rebuilding myself from dust, and I'm not sure I had the strength.

"Of course it was real. I loved you."

"When did you stop loving me and start hating me enough to ruin my life?"

He sighed as though I was taking up too much of his time with my pathetic questions. "I don't hate you, Amelia. You're being dramatic. I did what I did to keep my reputation and my job clean. There was no other way—"

"You could *not* have cheated!"

He ignored me. "I don't know when I stopped loving you. I think it happened over time. Perhaps when it became clear your work was more important to you than I was."

Just when I thought I couldn't be more offended, he came out with that nonsense. "*My* work? *My work?* Are you out of your mind? You're the one who was always at the hospital, answering calls every hour of the day and night, leaving me alone for days on end. And don't even *begin* to tell me your job is more important than mine." I held up a finger as he opened his mouth to interrupt before his lips curved into that smile again. "Or were you not really working those hours? Were you off screwing the brains out of your bimbo receptionist the entire ti—"

The sound of the slap echoed down the hallway, and I barely had time to put my hands out to stop my head from hitting the wall—such was the impact of his hit. Owen had *never* raised a hand to me, but apparently, all rules were out the door now. Fresh tears sprung in my eyes as I sunk to the floor, and Owen simply sighed again and glanced at his watch. When he reached out a hand to help me up, I shrunk back against the wall, pushing myself away from him. I couldn't stop looking at him, eyes wide with fear in realization of the monster in front of me.

Was I truly blind to him all these years?

Or had he changed?

Did it even matter?

Owen straightened his jacket and looked around the foyer. "I'm sorry that had to happen. I'm going to grab some things, then I'll leave. Read those papers. They have the details of our first consultation regarding splitting the assets. I suggest you get a lawyer."

I stayed curled against the wall, my forehead tucked against my knees while he moved around, grabbing things. I didn't care what he took—none of it mattered anyway. Everything in this house we'd bought together, and now all of it was simply objects attached to bad memories and a past with a man I apparently never knew.

He left, and I didn't look up, waiting to make sure he didn't come back before I dragged myself from the floor.

I made it to the bed, and for the second time that day, I cried myself to sleep.

CHAPTER
3

AMELIA

Smoothing my hands over my skirt, I uncomfortably shifted the long garment around my legs. The full-length mirror reflected a woman who looked sophisticated, chaste even, with a high-neck white top and a yellow skirt that billowed around my legs. With my spring boots on, no skin was showing apart from my hands and face.

And yet, when I met the hazel eyes of the woman staring back at me, all those nasty words that had been thrown at me this week slinked back into my mind, setting up permanent residence.

Whore.

Slut.

Bitch.

I deserved none of it, but the words took their toll, piling up around my shoulders and weighing me down until I started to wonder if I was wrong and the words were indeed true. I wasn't perfect. I didn't wait until marriage to have sex. Owen and I made love on our six-month anniversary in the back of his father's Mercedes. I'd only really committed myself back to the religion I was raised on *after* we got married, encouraged by Owen. Something about being back in the church for our wedding ignited my faith again, the building itself holding a magic I'd never been able to grasp in my hands but could hold in my heart.

The church community welcomed me.

Until they didn't.

The language they used to describe me was horrid as they'd texted and called, leaving messages on my voicemail when I refused to answer any of their attempts to speak to me. They used vile language that seemed entirely out of context with the religion that should be welcoming and forgiving.

And free of judgment.

It was Sunday morning, and I wanted to go to church even if I sat in the back pew instead of my usual seat three rows from the front and to the left, where the sun from the stained-glass window hit my lap at that time of the morning. I liked to watch the colors play across my skirt as I listened to the sermon. It reminded me to find magic in the smallest of places.

I needed to be cleansed of the nastiness that had plagued my life since Owen decided to use me as a scapegoat for his mistakes. It had only been a few days, but it might as well have been weeks, the hollowness inside me opening up and sucking me into its depths. I needed the comfort of the church and to feel God's presence around me because it felt like He had been siphoned from this house—a house that would no longer be my home soon enough. I didn't mind that part so much. I couldn't stay here anyway, not when everything in these walls dripped of Owen's tastes and style.

But my feet stalled as I stopped in front of the mirror in my bedroom. I couldn't seem to make them work to take one more step toward the front door so I could get into my car and to the salvation of the church and the community. If I didn't leave soon, I'd be late, and the large doors would creak as I opened them mid-service, and every head would turn my way, watch and judge me as I walked in.

No. I would get there earlier, find a quiet seat, and keep to myself.

Wrenching myself free of the invisible binds that seemed to be holding me there in place, I grabbed my purse from the hallway table and locked the front door, then slid into the driver's seat of my car. Again, I stalled, tapped my fingers against the steering wheel, and debated whether I should go. I shook my head rapidly, clearing the thoughts of doubt away. *No.* This was my church too. I had just as much right as anyone else to be there.

But as I pulled up in the church parking lot and stared through the windshield, my eyes went wide, and lips shook as I read the sign for today's sermon—*The Importance of Purity and Honesty.*

Visibly trembling, I summoned all my strength and stepped from the vehicle, keeping my head down and tucking a tendril of hair behind my ear that had come loose from the bun. Counting the cobblestones along the pathway toward the church, I didn't make eye contact with any of the congregation milling on the grass outside, stopping only when a shiny pair of heels came into my view, someone blocking me from entering the church.

"What are you doing here?"

Lifting my head, I was surprised I managed to

hold eye contact with the stern stare of Megan. She wasn't old enough to be my mother, though she acted like the unofficial mother of the church, bustling about as if it were *her* property and not a sanctuary for the community.

"I'm here for the service, Megan." I tried to smile but failed and instead focused on making sure I didn't cry. While all I wanted to do was break down and have someone tell me everything would be okay, my instincts were screaming at me not to show weakness. The hairs on the back of my neck tingled, and I strained to keep my gaze trained on Megan's face. Because it felt like every person was staring at me and slowly moving near me, either to surround me or block my entry, I wasn't sure.

Surely, it was my imagination.

"You're not welcome here anymore." She didn't add an insult to the end of her sentence, but the venom in her words was clear enough.

"The church welcomes everyone." My voice was small, unconvinced by my own words.

Father Brien appeared then at the top of the stairs, and I wanted to laugh in my relief and reach out to him. But something was wrong, and while his gaze wasn't cold like Megan's, it wasn't welcoming either.

I took a step back, my fears coming to the surface.

Just when I thought I would faint, Father Brien approached and offered me his arm. Automatically, I took it, leaning against him and seeking comfort in the only physical touch I'd had since Owen struck me two nights ago. "Walk with me, Amelia."

Grateful to get away from the leering crowd and hoping Father Brien would be able to ease the pain, I clung to him and let him lead me away from the church entrance.

"Things have been difficult," he started, and I nodded, staring at the ground again, watching my feet move over the pathway, feeling the hot tears stinging in my eyes. "There was a lot to consider." When I said nothing, he continued, "We have children in our community, Amelia."

I froze, and Father Brien stopped a beat after me, dropping his arm from mine. He wouldn't quite meet my gaze, instead glancing just above my eyes. I realized he'd been leading me back to my car, and I wanted to run away from the church, from everything. This place was meant to be my salvation, and I was being guided and *forced* away from it.

"Father, *please*. I need the church."

"I think it would be best if you found another church."

I grabbed his robed arm as he turned to leave, and for just a moment, there was pain evident in his eyes before it was gone and replaced with the same cold stare everyone was giving me behind his back. A stare they reserved just for me—*the town whore*. "Please, please don't do this. I *need* the church. Don't turn your back on me too."

"I have the community to think of, Amelia, and you are not the image we need."

"But—"

"I think it would be best."

All the fight left me, and I dropped my hand from his sleeve, watching helplessly as he moved back toward the church. I didn't move until everyone had gone inside, each one throwing me a look of sheer disgust before they did so.

What happened to no judgment?

What happened to acceptance?

Teenage memories resurfaced of me sitting on the grass outside the church, holding hands with a crying boy whose family had been ostracized from the church. I couldn't recall why, but I remember the anger that bubbled in my stomach as he spilled his story to me. We knew each other only from shared glances and smiles across the aisle, both happy to be where we were every Sunday.

Was that part of why I stopped going to church as a teenager? I had never lost faith, but I couldn't understand how a community that preached acceptance turned its back on some people.

And now *I* was one of those people, looking in from the outside, too dirty to be one of them.

Beyond saving.

Had I forgotten those teenage feelings of injustice so quickly? Just like I had not seen Owen for who he truly was? My God. Was I so stupid I couldn't see anything that was right in front of me?

Who was I?

Numbly, I turned and got back in my car. I'd taken a couple of days off work after everything was turned upside down and was due to go back tomorrow.

But what if they turned their backs on me too?

I'd need to move—a new town, a new job, a new church.

A new me.

But I didn't feel I had the energy for any of that.

Owen had taken everything from me, including the one thing I held dear...

... myself.

CHAPTER
4

AMELIA

For four days, I tried to fight my case at work, desperate to make my colleagues see my side of the story, but no *not one person* believed me.

Why would they?

When, in one corner, you have Owen, with his perfect smile and charm, apparently having spent years schmoozing everyone I worked with to be on his side if everything were ever to fail. And in the other corner of the proverbial boxing ring was me. Someone who, despite my best efforts, was still seen as mousey, quiet, and desperate for attention and validation from those who were above me. Apparently, they felt this extended beyond the office, and I was susceptible to doing *anything* for attention, including seeking out multiple sexual partners. It amazed me how quickly they put these thoughts together, and their opinion of me solidified purely because Owen got his story out first.

It was already too late to tell mine.

As I left the office on Monday afternoon, someone muttered, "It's always the quiet ones."

I wanted to scream.

The lunch room cleared every time I entered as though I were surrounded by poisonous gas, and conversation ceased whenever I walked into a room. The cubicles surrounding mine were eerily quiet, the sound of keyboards tapping and computer mice clicking louder than anything else as all friendly chatter ceased and was replaced with tense indifference.

Friday came, and I got wind by catching the end of a conversation before it had time to be stifled when they became aware of my presence—the monthly meeting had already been organized for this afternoon. I was usually pivotal in these meetings and hadn't been told the time or location.

I managed to summon enough fury to walk into my boss' office without knocking. "Greg," I started, forgoing polite formalities. Apparently, everyone was past that. "Why wasn't I told about the monthly meeting this afternoon?"

"Amelia." He folded his hands on his desk before he looked at me. I was getting tired of people saying my name as if I were a small child they were about to explain a simple concept to. "I think we need to talk."

"Are you going to ask me how *I'm* coping with all of this? Because the time for you to have been polite and caring was at the beginning of the week, not now."

"Amelia..." he started, once again saying my name in that irritating fashion. My anger at the tone he was using was enough to keep my fear at bay, even though terror was knocking at the back of my mind with increasing heavy-handedness. "You've done some amazing work since you've been here—"

"Thank you, but—"

"But," he said the word purposefully, his stare daring me to interrupt. "We are a marketing firm specializing in public appearance, keeping our clients' images our priority. This isn't a large town, Amelia. We're not New York, and our clients might not want someone representing their brand who's..."

I waited for him to finish, planting my hands on my hips and raising my brows. But he trailed off and made no attempt to find an adjective, so I spat out, "Who's a *whore?*"

"There's no need for such language in the workplace."

"Greg, you can't be serious!" I just about stomped my foot in frustration, and all I could see in my mind were images of Owen at work, with administration and the nurses flouncing about him.

Oh, poor Owen, whose wife cheated on him, what a dear.

Good thing he was able to find someone who loved him like Alison does.

She's such a good girl.

He did this, *all of this,* to save himself.

My marriage, my family, my friends, my church.

And now *my job.*

My anger faded in an instant, drowned out by hopelessness. I couldn't seem to hold onto the fight for long, and it would trickle through my fingers until I simply gave up and accepted my world was crumbling and let myself crumble with it. "You can't fire me."

Greg eyed me cautiously. "No, Amelia, I can't. Your personal issues are yours. But if no clients want you to represent them and your customer pool doesn't exist, then your position may become redundant."

"Is that a threat?"

"I'm merely explaining how it works in this industry and giving you a chance to leave on your own terms." I huffed out a humorless laugh at his words. *My own terms?* None of this was on my own terms. "We'll pay you for three months if you finish this week."

"Sounds like you and HR have already made your minds up."

"I'm sorry it had to be this way."

I didn't know what to say. What could I? What was the point in fighting a fight I was doomed to lose? Did I even care enough to try fighting? If I managed to keep this job, then what? Work with people who hated and judged me on someone else's story and be excluded forever. As I stood before someone I'd looked up to, who I thought cared about my well-being, the last flicker of my will to fight vanished.

I was nothing now.

Everything I thought I had that made me happy and made me who I was, was gone.

What's the point of fighting?

"Email me the papers," I mumbled and turned to clear out my desk.

Stepping out of Greg's office, the deep breath of air I took felt stale in my lungs, and my shoulders slumped further, deflated from all hope.

Terri approached me timidly as though she was afraid of being followed and touched my arm gently, lifting her chin to look into my eyes. "Amelia," she whispered, her voice shaking slightly. "I just wanted to say I'm sorry. I don't believe you did what everyone is saying."

A surge of warmth pumped through my chest, reigniting the hope I had lost. "Really?" The word came from my lips, desperate, filled with the force of my disbelief and anxiety that this lifeline might not be real. She nodded, her curls bouncing around her face, and I placed my hand on top of hers, where it rested on my arm. "Can you talk to everyone? If they know someone supports me, they might rethink."

Her gaze grew sad, and she slid her hand out from under mine, and I knew it was too late before she had even spoken. "I can't. I'm sorry. I don't want to risk my job. I just wanted you to know I support you."

My tone was cold, and she flinched as I said,

"Support me with words only, though." I didn't mean to sound as harsh as I did, and I hated treating the one person who had reached out with such cold indifference, but I couldn't help it. She'd offered me a lifesaver, only to take it away when I reached for it.

"I'm sorry," she whispered and returned to her desk.

Somehow her confession had only made me feel worse.

Revenge.

A word that held so much meaning.

And it became the only thing on my mind after another week at home, alone, in a house empty of warmth. A house I would likely lose after the meeting scheduled with our respective lawyers in a month. I had no one to call or talk to but still had the occasional insulting text pop up on my cell to remind me—*as if I could forget*—of my isolation and torment.

The idea of revenge began to seed and take root in my mind—it was the only thing that made sense. Once the idea sprouted—considering there was nothing left of me to fight it, no part of me remaining with faith, hope, or belief in the best of people—it spread and took over, souring me, taking the shadow I was, and darkening me further. I thought I didn't recognize myself after everything fell apart, but I was a complete stranger once I started thinking about revenge.

The thought was all-consuming, and everything else came second.

Every idea I had of beginning my life anew was drowned out by one thought, *Owen must pay for what he'd done.*

I'd never been a big drinker, but with my emotions swirling in a conflicting mess, the rage slowly became stronger and possessed me. My resignation from the situation was replaced with anger, and while I should be fueling that anger into rebuilding myself, I needed to numb the rage first. Memories were swirling with wrath, hate, and hurt, and all of it painted a picture of who I had wanted to be and how that was so incredibly different from who I ended up being.

Once the idea of revenge was planted, the thoughts I had following it frightened me. It was like every bit of anger I'd had over any small injustice over my entire life simply sat below the surface, bubbling and stewing, waiting for the moment to come forth with that one act that would break me open, and all the rage would come flooding out.

That moment had happened.

I dreamed of killing Owen.

I hated admitting that, even to myself, but I did. I had vivid dreams of sneaking into Alison's beautiful home, paid for by her parents or a past lover—who knew—and driving a knife through Owen's chest as he slept. Alison would wake screaming, and then I would too, shattered from the dream with the sound of my maniacal laughter echoing in my mind after I'd removed the knife.

I'd had dreams of hitting Owen with my car, stalking him after he left the hospital, and chasing him down while he screamed pleas for forgiveness over his shoulder before I crushed him against a tree or wall. The thoughts and dreams were Technicolor vivid, with the red of his blood splashing over me, staining me like a work of art.

This was why I started having a few glasses of wine at night. It wasn't much, but for someone who rarely drank, it was enough for the buzz of the alcohol to dim the thoughts and allow me some dreamless sleep.

But the thoughts never went away.

They only got worse.

I switched from gruesome fantasies to genuine planning of how I could make Owen suffer.

It wasn't fair there were no consequences for what he'd done when I'd done nothing to deserve his wrath. All the suffering was on me and none on him. I was the one who'd have to uproot my life and start afresh, carrying the scars of his actions, while he got to live the life he'd created for himself, simply cutting me out and replacing me with Alison.

I considered releasing the complete set of photographs that included Owen's face, showing everyone he was lying. But only he had copies. He wasn't stupid enough to leave that window of opportunity open. Then I thought perhaps I could get him to admit what he'd done on tape, but when he'd hit me, he'd planted the fear of him in my soul. If I slipped up and he discovered what I was trying to do, he would hurt me again.

It felt like he was untouchable.

I could take out my anger on Alison.

Was she aware of his plan and what he'd done?

What if she wasn't?

What if he'd fed her the same lies he had everyone else from the beginning?

I could sneak in and kill him, but was that enough? Would he suffer as I had? Or would it be over too quickly, and I would be left with the burden—whether I got caught or not—of living the rest of my life in a physical jail or a prison of guilt for taking a life?

Slouching against the couch, I absentmindedly swirled the remaining Shiraz around in my glass while my daydreams again switched between horrible things I could do to days before any of this had ever happened. I was barely paying attention to the three a.m. movie, but something about it caught my interest. The odd soundtrack, perhaps? A line of dialogue? I couldn't pinpoint the exact moment I went from staring over the top of the screen to focusing hard on the story, my hand over my mouth and eyebrows raised. Whatever it was, it was enough to cut through my tipsy blur until I was drawn into the story.

Was this even a thing?

Was this an option?

God, what was wrong with me?

Placing my wine glass down, I leaned forward and rested my elbows on my knees. The film was about a boy who'd been bullied in school and turned to summon the power of the Devil before using it to seek revenge on those who had wronged him.

I laughed a few notes of loud, potentially bordering on insane laughter.

Because what a ridiculous concept.

But even when the movie finished, I couldn't get the idea out of my mind.

And I couldn't sleep because the thought of summoning evil to seek my revenge was the stuff of movies. And *only* of movies. Of fiction.

By five a.m., curiosity had taken over me, and fully sober, I opened my laptop and delved down the rabbit hole to research witchcraft and the occult. I had no idea so many people followed Wiccan as a religion, and it seemed mostly peaceful, focusing on nature and empowerment through positive energy. Huffing out a note of interest, I dug deeper into exorcisms, looking beyond the movies and television shows and seeking information on summoning demons.

There were people who genuinely believed this was possible.

Did I believe it was?

And what would be the cost?

Would it take what was left of my sanity?

Or my soul?

The following afternoon I found myself in a small, dank bookstore, three towns over where no one knew my name or face, searching for books on demon traps and ritualistic summonings.

CHAPTER
5

AMELIA

The book was new, but I felt like it shouldn't have been. It should've had leather binding that creaked when opened to reveal thick and faded pages full of awful hand-drawn images, stained brown with old blood. Pages I'd needed to blow dust or brush debris off every time. Pages that held ancient evil.

At least, that's what these sorts of books always looked like in the movies.

Instead, the book sat unopened since I'd brought it home, its innocent red paperback cover staring unmoving at the ceiling from my dining table.

For two days, I'd eyed it suspiciously every time I'd walked through the room, then I'd shake my head and laugh, telling myself this was ridiculous.

Not only to have purchased the book in the first place but to be looking at it as though it would come to life and steal my soul.

But whenever I thought about it and the possibilities dark magic could open up to me, something would tug at the inside of my chest, calling me to it.

I tried to ignore the feeling, but even as I sat on the couch, unsure what else to do with my day but play games on my cell and surf the web, I found myself seeking out more sites on the occult and how to go about what I'd been planning, even as I tried to tell myself I hadn't been planning anything. I sought out general information at first, but every time I would end up diving into specific instructions on how to summon a demon. Because if I had the power to do such a thing, not only would I have my revenge, but then I'd have the power to get my life back on track. The idea of controlling a supernatural being was enticing, and I'd find myself staring at the wall intently as visions and possibilities swirled through my mind before I'd click my tongue impatiently.

Was I really considering this?

Perhaps, if nothing else, this could be a turning point for me. It was a line in the sand, an end to this life and the start of a new one, and a sign I was going to take control of my life—a life that had been so painfully torn from my grip. Maybe I could mold it into what I deserved all along, not the image I forced myself into to keep everyone else happy.

Maybe the demon was only metaphorical—an illusion created to kick-start me into taking back what was taken from me. The demon could be *me*. I could be summoning the strength I always wished I'd had, fighting my own fight. Even if it meant leaving everything behind and starting afresh—something I had considered many times in the past few days but couldn't seem to find the guts to even dig out my suitcase and begin packing.

Maybe I really needed this.

It seemed I'd already made up my mind.

CHAPTER
6

AMELIA

It was difficult not to feel ridiculous, kneeling on the floor in the middle of my kitchen, having drawn a large pentagram on the linoleum with red paint and a splash of my blood. My bandaged hand throbbed even as I remembered mixing the concoction. I'd been a wuss, looking away as I had cut into my palm with a knife. I struggled not to cry as I squeezed the cut, steadily dripping blood into the small pot of paint before stirring it rapidly, trying to hide my shame from myself. I had white candles at each of the star's five points, a small urn in the middle burning incense, and most importantly a photograph of Owen.

Basically, I took several points from different

webpages and books I'd read.

I knew there was no way this would work, not in the literal sense, anyway.

But I didn't need it to.

Something about simply *trying* made me feel powerful, as though these actions were the first step to claiming my life back. Maybe after I did this little ceremony, I would leave—pack up and move to another town. And I'd leave the evidence of my occult experiment on the floor for Owen to find and hope it haunted his nightmares and made him think I had put a curse on him. Maybe he'd wonder if he knew me all along as I now wondered about him. Maybe he'd think I was a witch, and I released a manic giggle at the thought that word would get around to my former church—a church that had abandoned me in my time of need.

Taking another gulp of wine, I cleared my throat and read the incantation out loud.

It was in Latin, *I think*, and I had to enunciate some of the words a few times, working my lips around the strange syllables. At the second paragraph, there was a gush of wind as the back door slammed open, making the candles flicker.

I screamed and then laughed.

Ridiculous.

As I moved forward with this ceremony I'd created, something was changing in me. It must've been a point of mind over matter. Perhaps I was so determined for a physical representation of the moment I took my life back that even kneeling here with the candles and paint was enough to make me feel I had the power to move forward.

Because I did feel it, as though the power was surging through my veins and tickling at the back of my neck like I was being watched. The feeling filled my chest and surged me forward until I was reading each word aloud with glee, crying them out, and smiling wide. The fact I was even *trying* this was a turning point for me. I could feel it and was almost overcome with the giddy urge to burst into laughter.

This was it.

This ceremony was no longer about raising a demon to seek revenge. *Was it ever?* Somehow this was what I needed, and I didn't question it. Instead, I embraced the sensation and let this newfound power fill me. This power I'd created for myself. Was it always there inside me? Had it been taken away from years of being told who I could be and what I could do?

I felt utterly amazing, better than I had in weeks,

years even, and better than I did *before* all this.

This was the beginning of the *new me*.

Grinning, I finished the incantation and raised the book above my head as I closed my eyes, taking in a deep, satisfying breath of the cool air that drifted through the open back door into the kitchen.

Nothing had happened.

No lightning strike.

No exploding thunder from outside.

No flickering lights.

No demon standing in front of me in the pentagram, trapped and waiting for instructions.

Nothing.

Sighing, I smiled. It was the first time I had truly smiled in so long, and I felt renewed. Maybe there was something to this stuff, and perhaps, as part of my new life, I'd leave the church behind and look into this instead. Or I could leave all organized religion behind and simply focus on myself and who I was inside. Wiccan wasn't for me either, I don't think, although I chuckled as I glanced at the pentagram on the floor. This wasn't Wiccan but some mishmash of random things I'd found thrown together in some vague attempt to kick me in the butt to *do* something.

Untucking my legs, I stood, careful not to lean in

the not-quite-dried paint. My little ceremony had been fun, which was odd, as all I'd done was sit still and read from a book. But I definitely felt different, and I wasn't going to question it.

I was going to go pack for my new life right now.

A cool breeze swept across my back, and I shuddered, wrapping my arms around my chest.

Guess it's going to be colder tonight than the weather forecast predicted.

About to turn to close the back door, I stopped when the breeze brushed past me again. But this was different. This wasn't the gentle touch of a cool spring breeze but slower, as though fingers of air were tracing lines across the back of my neck and over my shoulders.

My next shudder had nothing to do with the chill.

"You shouldn't mess with powers you don't understand, Amelia."

I whipped around, my hands coming up to clutch at my throat, unable to find any words and in deep shock, holding back the scream that threatened to escape.

The demon smiled at me, raised a hand, and placed a clawed finger on his lips, shushing me gently like a lover. The move was so gentle, so intimate, my knees almost buckled at the sensuality of the simple motion. A wave of heat hit me then as though I'd walked into a wall of it, and with it came his scent—masculine and carried by hellfire—as a thousand fingers caressed every inch of my skin, teasing me.

He looked human—mostly—if it weren't for the slightly curved red horns that protruded from his forehead, the orange glow to his eyes, and the long tail ending in an arrowhead point that lashed lazily against the floor. He was naked, gloriously so, and I desperately tried to keep my eyes trained on his and not let my gaze wander down over sculpted arms and abs to peek lower.

"You're not real," I whispered, stepping back. "There's no way it actually worked."

He huffed an amused breath, still smiling, and pushed himself from the doorframe where he'd been leaning before approaching me with graceful strides. "It didn't work, not quite. You had some elements right... the blood, for example, *your* blood." He licked his lips, and I twisted my hands together. The heat radiating from him was distracting. My mind began fogging from his sheer physical attraction, making it difficult to concentrate on anything else. I'd been attracted to Owen—he was a handsome man—but this *demon* was something else. It was an attraction on an entirely new level—pure, animalistic attraction that had me wanting to strip off my clothes right now.

Not just strip, but shred the fabric to pieces, expose myself to him in every way, and let him do anything he pleased.

I'd never felt that way, and it frightened me.

The demon took another few steps toward me, and I kept backing away until my back hit the wall. He reached out, placing one palm flat on the wall and blocking me into the corner with his body. God, I wanted to touch him to see if the heat from him was real and find out that if I ran my hands down his chest, would I get burned?

"I felt your *need* for me, Amelia," he whispered, brushing his lips along my cheekbone. I bit back a moan. He was deliciously hard, and I wanted to cling to him just to feel his body next to mine. If I could have only that, then the rest of these wicked thoughts would vanish. "Through the walls of Hell, I felt your need and desire for revenge. But it was more than that." He breathed in deeply, and when he released his breath, my hair fluttered around my shoulders. "You *called to me.*"

"Who are you?"

"You may call me Draven."

"Draven," I breathed out the word, almost panting. "I... I don't want you here. I don't need your help anymore."

He pressed his body against mine then, crushing me between the wall and his solid form, and I *moaned* at the sensation, biting my lip too late to stop the sound of desperation. Draven hadn't stopped smiling, fangs on display as I tried to hold contact with his orange eyes even as a flush crept over my cheeks.

Don't look away, Amelia.

Was I afraid if I looked away, he would disappear? Or he'd still be here when I looked again?

"Oh, but I think you *do* want me..."

My lips parted, and I leaned toward him instead of away, swaying on the tide of need for him, seeking to feel his mouth on mine. I did want him but not for revenge. The thought of getting back at Owen was a shadow of a whisper past my mind now that more depraved images had entered, replacing all else. My clit throbbed and ached, and I wanted so much for him to touch me and so much more.

When Draven licked his lips, I snapped my head back, forcing myself to concentrate and come to my senses. Ducking out from under his arm, I crossed the kitchen. "No, this isn't right."

Draven was on me in a second, closing the space between us and grabbing my hands, pressing them against the cupboards above my head and, once again, trapping my body next to his. His other hand traced down my spine, chuckling when I arched away from his touch, only to press myself against his naked body. Every breath he made shuddered like an echo bouncing around in my mind, sending shockwaves of pleasure through my body.

God help me.

I wanted more.

7

DRAVEN

"What do you want from me?" she asked, parting those deliciously delicate lips I looked forward to biting. She gasped when she noticed my fixation on her lips. She was so *close* it wouldn't take much to lean forward and swipe my tongue along her skin, tasting her. She'd open her mouth for me, accepting me. With the slightest touch, I could have her open her legs to welcome me too.

Soon...

So beautiful, so *innocent.*

I don't think I've ever had such an innocent before me, and I certainly never dreamed such a woman would summon me. I couldn't resist her call. I'd ignored others, allowing other demons to take the deals, but Amelia was mine from the moment her soul begged *please* with her need for power and revenge.

"You summoned me," I answered. "You offered me your soul in exchange for revenge."

And so much more, *so much more.*

She called to me, cried out for me, desperate, frantic, and eager for *me.* I felt Amelia's soul asking for help. She'd been beaten down and broken and felt loss so complete there was nothing left inside except her desire for revenge and for me, even if she didn't know it yet or was hesitant to admit it to herself. I would fill her life with pleasure she's never known, but there was a cost.

"My soul?" Her delicate throat bobbed as she swallowed. "So, after I die, I go to Hell?"

Yes, some deals worked like that, and others took years off your life as well, but not this deal, not for my Amelia. I set the terms. I chuckled, stopping when she bit her lip again. Oh, how I wanted to sink my teeth into her lip. I bet her blood would taste so sweet on my tongue. I glanced back at the pentagram she'd made. I'd gotten the barest essence of her blood from the scent of her ceremony, but it wasn't enough. I needed it from the source. I wanted to bite into her throat and take what I needed.

But first, business.

"You think your soul is simply something you sacrifice after you die? Something you don't have to think about between now and the moment you leave this mortal realm? No." Amelia squirmed against my hold on her hands. Maybe she hoped I wouldn't notice how she rubbed her thighs together and the distracted look in her eyes, begging me for release.

Soon, my kitten.

"You'll devote your life to me. You'll worship me. In turn, I'll worship you and your body however I desire." I wondered what she thought I meant and if she truly knew what I would do to her. If she was as innocent as I thought, the sex she'd had before me was *nothing* compared to what I would introduce her to. They'd called her a whore, and I felt it in her soul's cries to me. She'd be a whore but only for me. "From now until the darkness of eternity swallows us whole, in this realm and the next. You'll be mine."

"But—"

"So you have to ask yourself, my dear Amelia…" I lifted my hand, brushing past the mound of her breast, resisting the urge to flick over her erect nipple. There'd be plenty of time for that later. I held her gaze, full of uncertainty and conflicting arousal, as I traced a black claw down her cheek before cradling her face in my palm. "How badly do you want this revenge?"

There was a flicker of something in her pupils, and my fangs were exposed as I grinned again. Oh, she wanted revenge so badly that she would give *anything* to have it. I could provide it for her. I could torture the man who hurt her in ways she'd never dreamed of. But I wanted my payment—a taste of what she could give me forevermore.

And I always collected up front.

"Your soul may be calling to me, kitten, but I need your words." I brushed my lips along her other cheek, chuckling as she shuddered under my touch. "Then I'll take your body to seal the deal."

"Do you mean…"

"I'm going to fuck you, Amelia." Her resulting shudder and moan sent electricity coursing through my body. "I'm going to fuck you as hard and as long as I want. Then I'll seek your revenge."

She swallowed, her voice small. "And then?"

"And then you're mine. Forevermore. *Mine.*"

She was nodding, and I wasn't even sure she knew she was doing it. Amelia bit her lip again as her mind ran through everything she'd been through, cementing what she already knew. She deserved revenge, and I was the only one who could give it to her. I was practically in her head, feeling what she felt, knowing what she desired. The woman she was a few weeks ago was gone. She's stronger now, even if she didn't know it yet.

I would show her how much stronger.

"Yes," she said, her tongue darting out to wet her lips. "I accept."

Without another word, I dived forward, gripped her hands harder, claimed her mouth with mine, and sealed the bond.

CHAPTER
8

AMELIA

My eyes widened as Draven kissed me before I let them flutter shut, whimpering under the ministrations of his tongue. His hand had already left my cheek and was wandering down, palming my breast. I couldn't stop trembling, unable to control the surges of desire that pulsed through me. Nothing was on my mind except Draven and his very naked body pressed against me, my clothes in the way between the heat of his skin and mine. He held me still while he swirled his tongue around the inside of my mouth, tasting, teasing, and showing me what he could do to me with a simple kiss that almost had me begging for more on the spot.

My chest was yanked forward as he grabbed my

top, and I screamed into the kiss as he shredded the fabric, finishing by snapping open my bra in the center with a *snick* of the talons on his fingers. The fabric fell to the side, hanging limply and exposing me to him. I automatically squirmed, my instinct to cover my body from view. It was too bright in this room. I didn't remember turning on the light, but the sharpness from the globes drowned out the gentle light from the candles. There was nowhere to hide, and I squirmed, trying to sway the remnants of the fabric to cover my breasts. I stilled when he growled and slowed the kiss, enticing me again to submit to him, promising pleasure and danger and humming when I melted against his touch as his claws tickled my skin.

"That's it, Amelia. Let me inside your mind... let me take your body." His whispers were delicate brushes against my cheek and neck, and his following words had me trembling, and I couldn't stop. "I'm going to fuck you so hard, kitten." He kissed me again, dragging his teeth along my bottom lip until I tasted the metallic tang of blood.

"Shouldn't we..." I gasped, breathing against his cheek as he broke the kiss long enough for me to speak. I ran my tongue over the inside of my lip, my brows furrowing at the taste of blood. Droplets were on his lips, and he snarled as he licked them off, sending another wave of shivers down my spine. I wanted him, but I wanted to relish in the feel of him, a desire so strong it pushed all other thoughts from my head that this should be savored. The chill of the breeze against my exposed nipples reminded me of my semi-nudity. It was happening too quickly. "Shouldn't we slow down a bit?"

A deep laugh rumbled through his chest, and he thrust his hips forward, pressing my lower back painfully against the counter and rubbing his erect length, already sticky with precum, against my bare stomach. "This isn't a date, kitten. This is a deal. There'll be plenty of time later for me to take my time with you."

"L-later?" I couldn't think straight. *Had we discussed this?* I was intoxicated by his presence. Somewhere in the back of my mind, the warnings of the lure of evil were swimming around, but the heat of him drowned them out, need pooling between my thighs.

"After I've sought your revenge, then I'll come back for you and take you again." He ran his sharp teeth down my earlobe, and I shuddered. "And again, and as many times as I want. Your body is mine, not just your soul." His breath left his body in one long note of satisfaction as I whimpered. Draven whispered against my ear, leaving me wondering how something so quiet could be the loudest thing I'd ever heard. "You're going to be such a good kitten for me, aren't you?"

I gasped again, stretched onto my toes, and ground my hips against Draven. The ache in my clit was too distracting, and the friction alluded me. I wanted to beg him, and I *needed* him to touch me. He was right—there was plenty of time later. Of course, he was right. How could I have wanted anything else but him inside me?

"Say it, Amelia," he growled out. *How did he know what I was thinking?* "I want to hear you say it."

"Draven," I whispered, curling my hands into fists and tugging against his hold on my wrists. He didn't let go, and his orange eyes glowed with a fierce intensity as he waited for me to speak. To confess what I wanted in a way I had never done before, to say it out loud. "I want you to fuck me, Draven. *Please.*"

With a snarl, his teeth found my neck, and I cried out as he bit down, stopping just short of drawing blood and instead sucking hard, bruising and weakening the skin until blood pooled at the surface and the slightest nick from his teeth would pull it free. He tilted his head, piercing the skin with his fang, and I cried out, tugging hard against his grip on my hands. His mouth found my neck, his tongue dragging hot lines across the skin and lapping up the steady droplets of blood. I sighed as the pain eased, and I was left only with the sensation of his mouth on my skin.

Draven released my wrists, and I stretched my throbbing fingers, barely having the time to get feeling back in my hands before bracing myself against the counter as he bent to yank my pants down. He crouched before me, inhaling deeply before pressing his tongue to the outside of my cotton panties. I moved to clutch his head and found horns and gripped them as he flattened his tongue against my clit. Squirming against his touch, I moaned. Even the thin fabric was too much of a barrier. He lowered my panties, guiding me to step out of them, his breath hot against me.

Draven was on his feet again, smirking as I fell apart under his touch.

I didn't want to wait any longer.

"Shall we go to the bedroom?" I asked, feeling foolish as I took in the demon in front of me. I finally allowed myself more than a glance at his cock and choked back a cough at the size of it. Nine inches of thickness, and I dared to reach out and trace my fingertips over the lines of veins, imagining them rubbing inside me. Withdrawing my hand, I flushed when he chuckled.

"So innocent," he muttered and bent to grab my ass before lifting me onto the counter, spreading my legs so he could stand between them. "I look forward to destroying you."

Draven grabbed his erect cock and fisted it a few times before running the head up and down between the wet lips of my pussy. I cried out, gripping his shoulders when the head hit my oversensitive clit, my legs trembling when he did it again. He chuckled, his signature sound so calm when I was falling apart. "So wet for me." He grabbed my hips and slid me to the edge of the counter before pressing his cock against the entrance of my pussy. I waited for him to push, bracing myself on the counter, ready for the slick drag of him inside me.

Draven smirked, the pause enough for me to look at him with my eyebrows raised, waiting. He penetrated me with a grunt and hard thrust, causing me to scream at the invasion. Whimpering and squirming, I instinctively tried to get away from the discomfort of the intrusion. His claws dug into my skin as he gripped my hips, holding me still and ignoring my attempts to move away. He didn't wait, simply chanting, "Yes, yes," as he held onto me and fucked me ruthlessly, my legs shaking from the force.

Slowly, the ache eased, and I lifted my legs to wrap them around his hips. "Yesss…" he hissed out. With a grunt, he lifted me from the counter, bouncing me up and down on his thick cock with ease as though I weighed nothing to him.

"Oh God, *Draven!*" He chuckled again, grunting as he thrust harder, lifting and using me. His tongue licked against my earlobe, and I gasped. My body was his to use and devour, and I resisted the urge to go completely limp in his arms, to force him to hold me upright or simply let me sag and continue to use me. The dull ache in my clit had grown to an intense throb, and every slight brush past the bundle of nerves was enough to make my legs jerk. I was close, the coil of pleasure twisting and ready to snap inside me, and I hadn't even touched myself yet.

"You're going to come for me, my kitten." It was a command, and I nodded, knowing the slightest touch would set me off, but would it be enough to ease the ache of need?

Forevermore.

Draven snatched my hand and threw it back over his shoulder before bending forward slightly so the back of my thighs pressed against his hip bones as he tilted me, reaching deeper.

I mewed in protest. I couldn't reach myself from this angle. "I need to touch my—"

"No, you don't." His words were like honey, filling me with his darkness as he pounded into me. "You're going to come just like this." He jerked into me with long, deep thrusts that dragged against my inner walls. I couldn't stop shaking, but even without contact against my clit, my peak drew closer, and he smirked as my eyes widened. "Just like this…" he muttered.

I wanted to argue and tell him I couldn't come without touching my clit. But his voice alone was working magic against me with the heat of his touch, his fingers searing against my ass as his claws dug into my skin. His breath against my neck was calm and collected while he fucked me harder and deeper. Draven's intake of breath was a shudder against the air, and every other sound drowned out as the atmosphere around me was sucked away until nothing was left but the power of his command.

I jerked in his arms.

"Come."

All at once, the pleasure hit harder and more intense than I was prepared for, sending shockwaves through my body as my legs shook and I screamed his name.

Draven laughed then, pushing me past my limit as he resumed his violent pace, and I clung to him, panting and whimpering.

I came down from my high—almost—the pleasure never stopped as he kept thrusting into me, and I squeezed his shoulders, resting my face against the crook of his neck. "I want you to come…" I muttered. And I did. I wanted him to have even more pleasure than he'd given me. I wanted everything for him.

Squeezing my eyes shut, I fought back the urge to cry that threatened to overwhelm me, abruptly feeling as though I wasn't enough for Draven. Surely, there were women out there who could give him more, who *were* more than me? If penance for my summoning him was pleasure, a twist in my chest told me it was fundamentally wrong, like there should be consequences for my actions.

But good doesn't always win, does it?

My thoughts or his? I couldn't tell.

A rumble ran through Draven's chest. "I will

come, but I'm not done with you yet."

Before I could ask, he shifted, pulling out of me with a slick sound and lowering me to my feet. My legs trembled, and I leaned against the counter, unsure if I could stand. He said nothing, but smirked again as he scooped his hands under my arms and let me sink to the floor to kneel as my legs turned to jelly under me.

Draven walked away, his large feet sounding loudly against the cool floor, and I reached out for him as he passed me. He turned when he was a handful of steps away, cocking an eyebrow at my outstretched hand. "Don't worry, kitten. I'm not going anywhere." The fire burned in his eyes again, and he moved to the middle of the pentagram I had painted what felt like eons ago. "I want you to come to me."

I eyed his cock, erect and bobbing slightly as he straightened, and when his hand encompassed the length and started pumping, it forced the breath from my lungs as need overtook me. Reaching up, I slapped a palm against the counter, prepared to use it to heave myself to my feet.

"No kitten, not like that." He hadn't raised his voice, but I still obeyed as though he had, withdrawing my hand from the counter and remained kneeling on the floor, staring at him.

Waiting for my next instruction.

"Good girl." The praise sent a shudder down my spine, a kink I either didn't know I had or one that had never been pulled to the surface before Draven. "Crawl to me."

Pushing myself onto my hands and knees, I shoved away the lingering hesitation, the part of me saying *not* to obey, to move to my feet and stand because crawling was…

Drogatory.

Submissive.

Erotic…

I crawled, and Draven chuckled, holding my eye contact, and I crossed the threshold into the pentagram. He pounced, grabbed my head and shoulder, and forced my face against the paint, smearing it along the floor and my skin. Positioning himself behind me, he penetrated me again, snarling as I moaned.

As Draven set a steady pace with his thrusts, he asked, "Have you ever taken it up the ass, Amelia?"

I clenched around him, twisting around to stare at him. "No."

"Good." He chuckled, twisting his hand into my hair and tugging. "So, I get to take your virginity." I choked out a protest, and he smiled. "Not tonight, don't you worry. But soon, I'll have you begging me to fuck your virgin ass."

"But—"

Again, I couldn't finish my sentence as Draven changed the angle, planting a foot next to my head and forcing my face to the floor again. He pressed in deeper, the kitchen filled with the obscene sounds of sex and the scent of my arousal.

Draven started snarling like an animal was taking over, and this time when he made the command, he was panting, "Come for me."

I did, convulsing, unable to think, and simply braced myself against the floor and the intensity of his thrusts, submitting and taking everything he had to give. The stretch was no longer a discomfort but something I wasn't sure I could live without now I'd had a taste.

A voice whispered in my mind, and again I wasn't sure if it was his or mine.

You don't have to live without—you're his forevermore.

I groaned, my sex tightening around him as my orgasm surged, my clit tingling with sensation even though I wasn't touching myself. It was his voice. He could *command* me to come without even a brush against my clit. I clenched around him again at the thought, and he grabbed my hair, leaning forward to whisper closer to my ear, "You've figured it out, haven't you, kitten? How I can make you scream without even touching you?" I moaned. There was nothing else to say. "There are so many things I want to do to you. I look forward to tying you down and making you come over and over until you're sobbing and *screaming* for me to fuck you."

My legs trembled, on the edge of absolute pleasure again. Too late, I realized I didn't want this to end and almost sobbed at the idea of him stopping his thrusts. The pleasure of Draven was all-consuming, touching every part of me inside and out. The heat of him, the pricks of pain from his claws, the sound of his tail thrashing against the cupboards and floor as his thrusts became sporadic—he was going to come.

"No," I sobbed out, gripping against nothing as my fingers tried to clench against the smooth floor, getting only smears of paint on my forearms and palms. "Don't stop."

Between his growls, there was another laugh, and he sped up, the slapping of his sack against my clit the only touch needed to send me over the edge again, the ache replaced with pleasure as I came. I cried out, *"Please!"* my tone thick with the desperation that pulsed through me. I wanted his cum, I wanted it inside me, but I didn't want him to stop, now or ever. Any hesitation I had was replaced by sheer ecstasy, and I tried to cling to the sensation as I gripped harder around him, willing him to keep going forever.

"Those things you're feeling, kitten, that *need* for me... that's the deal being sealed. You're mine."

"Yes..."

"Say it," he barked out, gripping harder, grabbing the flesh of my ass in his hands.

"I'm *yours.*"

With a snarl, he came, the heat from his cum spilling inside me as he slowed, pushing his seed deeper into me.

Whatever he wanted, I would give him.

I submitted myself fully to the demon.

I was *his.*

CHAPTER 9

DRAVEN

Amelia passed out in my arms, the scent of sex thick around us as my seed spilled from her sweet cunt, swollen and twitching. I brushed my fingers through the wet folds, and she whimpered even through her sleep.

So many things I would do to her.

I would wake her from slumber with my cock in her cunt, her mouth, or pushing past the resistance of her tight asshole. I'd lick her until she begged me to stop, then restrain her and keep going. I wanted to taste her cum when she was too exhausted to give more.

A satisfied growl rumbled through my chest as I glanced over my shoulder at the remains of her shredded clothes. I would shred all her clothes—she wouldn't need them with me.

But it was time to seek her revenge.

Lifting Amelia, I stood, hooking my arms under her shoulders and knees. She sighed and tucked her head against my chest, making me pause and tilt my head—such an affectionate move and not one I deserved. I owned her now, but I wondered if she truly realized what that meant. Few went into a deal with a demon, completely understanding the full extent of the deals made. Most were too keen for their reward, too distracted by the blessing they sought to pay attention to the fact they were paying for it with their blood and souls. Humans were fickle and would often sacrifice parts of themselves they didn't fully understand simply to have things they thought were impossible or not within their grasp.

For Amelia, it was revenge, and I think that's why her call found me, and I couldn't let it go. She was my first and would be my only deal. Humans made deals for all sorts of reasons—riches and talent or love and companionship. But *revenge?* It wasn't as common as I would have assumed during my experience with humanity. Humans were selfish creatures, mostly, and for your innermost desire to be to inflict pain on someone else…

No wonder I was drawn to her call.

Amelia's summoning had been sloppy, amusing at best, but enough to get my attention, to tug at my chest rather than the twist and grab, which was a correctly-conducted ceremony. I felt her across the walls of Hell.

A delicate soul, pure and innocent.

So naïve.

And inside that soul was the darkness calling, a darkness born from pain she never knew herself capable of feeling. She didn't want respite from the pain and wasn't asking for riches or even happiness. No, my Amelia was asking for those who hurt her to feel the pain she had.

I'd enjoy tearing Owen apart.

But not physically—at least not at first. That would be too simple, and Amelia deserved more from me. I'd put Owen through agony, make his heart and soul ache, and make him *beg* for death to spare him from a suffering he couldn't free himself from.

Then I'd do it again.

Then *maybe,* if I was feeling generous, I'd make him hurt physically as a finale. Amelia would then be mine, and I'd take her home with me, keep her as my kitten.

My delicious fucktoy.

Looking down, I took a moment to admire her naked body as I kicked the door to the bedroom open. Her breasts shifted with my movements, and my tongue darted out to wet my lips at the pink tips of her nipples, erect from the cold. *Or perhaps, erect because of me.* I preferred that thought.

She was smooth and delicate and snuggled farther into me as I tried to lay her on the bed. Her hands curled around my neck, and I chuckled, dropping her onto the mattress when being gentle didn't work. She woke with a grunt.

Her eyes opened sleepily, and she reached for me, making grabbing motions with her hands toward my horns as I leaned over her. "Are we going to have sex again?" Amelia was pleading already, wanting more, and I was tempted to let her grab onto my horns and steer my face between her silky thighs.

I barked out a laugh at her neediness and maneuvered her so I could tuck her legs under the sheets. Her brows drew together as she let me, no doubt confused by my compassion. But she was my kitten, and I wouldn't hurt her, not outside the discipline she required when it came to fucking. I noticed her hesitation when I demanded she crawl to my feet. It wouldn't take long to fuck that out of her, to spank her until she understood she was my kitten. "No, my sweet. You're going to sleep, and I'm going to go pay Owen a visit."

Amelia sat up abruptly, letting the sheet fall to her waist. I didn't try to disguise my eyeing her, and she didn't shy away from my attention. Her eyes were wide and wild, and I pressed my palms to the mattress, leaning forward so we were eye to eye and breathing in the adrenaline from her. "You're excited," I whispered, glancing between her pupils, blown out with passion.

She looked down, shying away from the darkness in her that leaped with excitement at the idea of Owen's suffering beginning. A flush crept up her neck, and her shoulders stiffened as she whispered, "What are you going to do to him?"

"What would you like me to do to him?" I purred out the words, letting my breath brush over her ear, chuckling when she shuddered and arched her back to push her chest toward me.

"I want…"

"You can tell me, Amelia. Nothing you say will make me desire you any less."

She again made eye contact, but confusion laced

her expression between her other conflicting thoughts. She wanted Owen to suffer. I could feel it practically radiating from her. However, she was human and intertwined with those dark thoughts that drew me to her was uncertainty.

"I want him to hurt like I hurt."

I nodded, absorbing her words and reveling in the small gasp she made as I traced my claws along her cheek.

"Do you know what he did to me?" She shuddered, tears beginning to brim in her widened eyes.

"I know everything."

"I don't think..." She took a deep, steadying breath, lifting her gaze to mine and tilting her head against my palm. *So innocent.* "I don't think I want you to kill him."

"I won't kill him. Death is too good for the likes of him."

"Promise?"

Another chuckle rumbled through my chest. "I promise, my kitten. Where would the fun be in that?"

When Amelia opened her mouth to respond, I snaked my fingers around the back of her head, drawing her toward me for a kiss. I devoured her mouth hungrily, swallowing her whimpers and moans. I wanted her to be dripping wet when I came back. We might be apart for days, for as long as I deemed it fit to teach Owen a suitable lesson for how he hurt my Amelia. When I came back, she would be sore in all the best ways. I would fuck her for hours, make her come until she begged for mercy.

Then do it again.

I pulled away from the kiss, inhaling deeply as she was left breathless. Shifting off the mattress, I moved toward the door. "Stay at home. Don't go out. Don't talk to anyone. I'll be back." When I reached the door, I turned to find her still sitting in bed, clutching the sheet to her chest. "Amelia?"

"Yes?"

It was impossible not to smile every time she spoke in such an innocent tone with no malice. It made my cock hard to think of all the depraved thoughts of revenge she'd had, all the dark things that hid behind those bright eyes. All the things I would do to her.

Soon.

"Does Owen want children of his own?"

"Yes, that was one of the reasons we—" Her eyes flicked to mine. "Wait, why are you asking?"

My eyes flashed as I smiled, exposing my fangs. "I'll see you soon, my kitten."

Her second cry of, "Why are you asking?" was cut off as I slammed the bedroom door behind me and disappeared in a wisp of smoke.

CHAPTER 10

AMELIA

Using my hands, I pushed myself from the bed and sprinted after Draven, ignoring the fact I was naked. Usually, I wouldn't move about the house like this, even when alone—it felt sinful and exposed me to the world. Every flaw and imperfection I could count were on display, and even in my eyes, I was judged. But my nudity hardly seemed important anymore, and considering my skin was still burning warm from Draven's fingers and mouth, the idea of clothes made me squirm with discomfort.

"Draven?" I wrenched open the door, moving down the short hallway and circling the other rooms when he didn't answer. Stopping in the middle of the kitchen, I halted, my thoughts of *surely he couldn't have left that fast* were a harsh reminder Draven wasn't human.

Sighing, I grabbed a glass and filled it from the tap, trying to ignore the shaking of my hands as Draven's dark voice echoed through my mind.

Does Owen want children of his own?

"Dammit!" The glass shattered as I dropped it in the sink, and I stared at the broken pieces for a moment, not moving and gripping the counter until my knuckles turned white.

I could only think of one reason Draven would ask such a question.

My lip twitched into a smirk before I gasped, spinning around and slapping a hand over my mouth. No. I couldn't be *happy* at the idea of Owen's suffering. What kind of person would that make me? But when I dragged my hand from my lips and flexed my fingers by my side, I was still smiling. I had called to Draven across the realm of the world I thought I understood into one ruled by darkness.

Draven was going to make Owen suffer for what he did to me, to make him hurt the way I had, and that made me feel... *good.*

The recognition and acceptance also acknowledged that the pain in my life was I n the past.

Owen would hurt the way I *had* hurt, not the way I still did. While there remained a stinging ache in my chest, and if I pressed my hand over my heart, I could almost feel it, but it was dulled.

Darkened by Draven's presence and promises.

By our deal.

The power I'd felt during the ceremony still trickled through me, and I didn't think I could sleep. The thoughts of Owen's punishment sent a manic giggle to my lips, and again I slapped a palm over my mouth.

I hated the part of me that sought solace in Owen's pain, but I couldn't seem to shake it. Owen had ruined my life, taking *everything* from me to save himself—my family, church, job, marriage, and even my sense of self—and there had been no consequences for him. He would live the rest of his life happy, maybe have a family with Alison. Or perhaps she was only temporary until he found someone even younger and easier to manipulate.

Because that's what he'd done to me, wasn't it?

My brows furrowed as our years together slid past my mind's eye, every interaction and conversation now playing in a new light. He was a master manipulator to the point I didn't even realize what he was doing to me until he took everything away. I'd been given the illusion of freedom without ever really having any. I no longer spoke to my friends from college, and I recall they never liked Owen. He turned me against them, said they were jealous and they'd fill my mind with poison. My anger jumped up another notch after I remembered when I'd been offered a higher-paying job in another state, but Owen didn't want to move, convincing me it was a bad idea and that I should work for the smaller firm here with less pay.

So *he* had the upper hand.

The only thing he couldn't manipulate from me—*children.*

It wasn't something we discussed before we got married, and maybe we should have because I wanted to focus on my career. If—and it was an if—later, I decided to have a family, then good. If not, that was fine too. Owen couldn't *force* me to get pregnant. I had a contraceptive implant, so his refusal to wear a condom did nothing.

So, he went elsewhere and punished me for not being as compliant as he wanted.

Owen was penalizing me for wasting his time

and not being the wife he wanted me to be.

I was never a particularly strong person, but it turns out my *one* act of willpower had been the undoing of my relationship, and while I *hated* how he had done it, maybe it was for the best. I saw his true colors, but unfortunately, I had seen them too late.

Now I had Draven.

My pussy throbbed at the thought of the demon, and I ducked my head against my chest, knowing I was blushing without needing to feel the warmth on my cheeks with my fingers.

Had summoning him *really* been an accident?

I'd been in such a pit of despair I was willing to try anything to get my life back on track. Part of me had really hoped it would work. Draven said I called to him, that the ceremony I performed may have opened the line of communication, but it was the desire in my soul that drew him to me—the desire for revenge.

I had traded my soul to make Owen pay, and I didn't regret it.

Perhaps I should, but I simply couldn't find it in me to care. Something inside me had snapped and ripped from me when Owen had torn my life apart and replaced it when Draven appeared in my house.

Owen had shredded who I thought I was, and in place of who I had been, someone else stepped in.

Someone stronger with less regard for consequences.

Someone who simply wanted him to suffer for what he'd done.

Who's to say he wouldn't do the same to Alison?

That man needed to pay.

Smiling, I straightened, leaving the broken glass in the sink to clean up later. I glanced at the smeared pentagram on the floor, looking down to notice a streak of paint against my forearm where Draven had pushed me into the floor as he fucked me, and lifting a hand to my face, it came back with dried flecks of paint. I needed a shower, but I was hesitant to wash away the feeling of Draven on, in, and around me, touching every part of my soul and body.

But he'd be back to fill and mark me again.

I felt no regrets.

My shoulders dropped when a wave of exhaustion took over, and my eyelids fluttered as my body screamed for sleep it hadn't needed a moment before. I dragged myself to the bathroom for a shower before collapsing in bed, smiling to myself.

I'd promised my body and soul to Draven, and while I didn't know the fate that awaited Owen, the only emotion I could summon was anticipation for Draven to return to me.

CHAPTER
11

DRAVEN

Owen lived with Alison, their home located insultingly close to my Amelia's, and I scowled while stalking the perimeter of Alison's house. This man, if you could call him that, didn't deserve to be on the same Earth as Amelia, let alone within a few blocks.

The house was expensive and much too large for one person. Had it been left to Alison by family? A gift from another wealthy man she fucked out of his money? I resolved to find out. I needed to know if Alison deserved punishment too, or if she were simply another pawn in Owen's game.

Rounding the corner, I didn't bother to disguise the sounds I made, almost hoping Owen would look up and see me passing the window in the semi-darkness between street lights. I'd allow myself to be visible only to him. So when he caught a glance, no one else would see the monster.

Let the mind-fucking begin.

But he didn't look up because they were busy fucking on the couch.

Alison was squealing like a whore, and Owen's face reddened as he pumped up into her supple body, his hand gripping the back of her neck as she straddled him.

She was faking it. The sensations of pleasure ebbing from the couple were skewed drastically in his direction, and I chuckled, wondering if she regretted bringing him into her life. *Doubtful*. He was rich with a good job and reputation. He could offer her a stable life where all she needed to do was play the obedient housewife and fuck in exchange for a life of comfort.

After they finished, they moved upstairs, and I waited somewhat patiently until the sounds of their breathing that whispered through the air had steadied before I disappeared into smoke again, reappearing in their bedroom. Standing at the edge of the mattress, I watched them for a moment. Owen was in a peaceful slumber, as was his squeeze.

For now.

Prowling to his side of the bed, I bent down and placed my fingertips against Owen's forehead, smiling as his brow furrowed under the brush of my skin on his. If I didn't have Amelia, I might seduce Alison right now and wake Owen to witness me fucking her, forcing orgasm after orgasm from her right next to him while he remained frozen and unable to stop me. I'd show him what Alison's face looked like when she came hard, knowing he'd never be able to replicate it.

Releasing him from my gentle hold, I smiled.

Everything will be different for you tomorrow, Owen, and I'll be here to enjoy the show.

CHAPTER 12

OWEN

Tugging the blankets out of Alison's grip, I rolled over, groaning. The little minx always stole the blankets at night. How could someone so small and dainty have that much strength in her sleep? She'd roll back and forth until the blankets were tucked under and around her, and shifting them was next to impossible.

Facing her, I watched her sleep for a moment, my cock stirring at the sight of her—no lines around her eyes or mouth, her artificially filled lips slightly parted, a mouth waiting to be filled with cock and cum. The blanket swelled over her generous chest, and I smirked, knowing beneath the cocoon of warmth she'd created, her delicate waist led to her slick, warm cunt. Always ready for me.

Young. Impressionable. Beautiful.

And really fucking good at sucking cock.

She was the perfect woman.

Alison made a muffled grumble in her sleep as I dipped my hand under the blankets, brushing against her arm with my cool fingers. The covers were up to her nose, and when I pressed my hand between her thighs and pushed two fingers inside her, her brow furrowed as the blankets shifted, and she gasped. But she didn't wake, and I took a moment to pump my fingers into her before glancing at the alarm clock—*September 19, 5:15 a.m.*

Shit. No time to fuck, or I'd be late to work.

Also, my birthday was approaching. I hated the reminder I was aging, but I could usually sway it my way to get extra compliments. Petty? Maybe. I didn't care.

Alison's sigh as I removed my hand made me chuckle, and with another sleepy grumble, she burrowed deeper into the blanket tunnel she'd created around herself. When she rolled over, and all I could see was the disheveled waves of her dark, chestnut hair peeking out, she could almost be Amelia.

Ah, my dear Amelia. I hadn't thought of her often in the past few weeks, but when I did, it was with a wisp of emotion. I would thank her, in my mind, for being the sacrifice so I could have my cake and eat it too. My only regret was striking her the night I went to collect a few more of my things. But I wasn't going to stand still and allow her to toss nasty words at me—I deserved more than that. A shove would've done the trick, knocking her off her feet just as effective for the shock value.

Shrugging a shoulder, I pushed myself off the bed and stalked to the bathroom for a quick shower before my shift.

As I stepped out of the shower, wiping the fog from the mirror with my hand, I cried out.

What. The. Fuck.

Leaning forward, I brushed my fingers through my hair, and my hand came away full of short, dark hair. The patch created a receding hairline that wasn't there last night, and when in panic, I did it again, and another clump followed, exposing a bald patch above my ear.

Cursing under my breath, I glanced around wildly, storming to the bedroom to grab my cell.

Wait.

No need to call anyone. Andrew at the hospital

would be able to help or, at the very least, point me in the direction of someone who could. No need to panic. This wasn't something that couldn't be fixed by throwing money at it.

My cell buzzed in my hand, and I frowned at the notification.

Amelia's sister.

Isabelle: *You asshole. How long did you think it would be before the truth came out? Amelia told me everything and even has proof you were cheating first. I'm just sorry I didn't believe her. We're going to drag you through the courts. It's over.*

Proof? *Proof?* What fucking *proof* did Amelia have of anything? Only I had the original pictures of us that showed my face, and they'd been destroyed, wiped from my laptop, and a new hard drive installed, physically destroying the old one. No way, not possible, no chance. I hadn't messaged or emailed anyone with my plans—I wasn't that stupid. The only person who knew was Alison, given it was a plan we concocted together. Amelia cheating first was the leverage I needed to sway the divorce lawyer's opinion in my favor. I made more money than her, always had, and I was studying when we met, so she *knew* I was going to be well-off.

But *proof?*

Her sister wouldn't lie—what would be the point? She had something on me.

Sweat prickled at the back of my neck and my palm where I held my cell, still warm from charging overnight.

Glancing at the phone again, the time lit up on the locked screen at my touch—*5:45 a.m.*

Fuck!

No time to sort it out now.

Dressing, I shoved a beanie on my head and shrugged on a jacket so the beanie stood out less as a fashion choice and stormed out the door, my heart racing.

Andrew couldn't figure out why I was losing my hair—several more clumps fell to his office floor when I removed my beanie, drawing a moan from my throat. Afterward, I'd kept a cap on most of the day and managed to avoid any questions, setting up an appointment with a specialist Andrew recommended for the next day. Emergency appointments—the kind you only get through knowing the right people. Thank fuck for that.

Leaving my shift early, I'd been unable to concentrate after the message this morning from Amelia's sister, my mind racing through every possibility. I couldn't think of a single thing she could have on me, but being dragged through the court system with proof I'd set up the entire thing would bring everything I'd planned crashing down.

Arriving back at Alison's, I closed the door gently with a click, leaning against the thick wood and sighing to myself, trying to regain some composure. My fingers twitched as I resisted the urge to run my hand over my head, my stomach dropping at the thought of the bald patches hiding under my beanie. Would I be completely bald by morning? Could Andrew's recommendation even save me then?

Fuck.

Frowning, I pushed myself from the door, tilting my head.

Someone was here.

The familiar sounds of fucking became clearer as I ascended the stairs, Alison's moans gone porn-star level for whoever this asshole was with her. Shoving the bedroom door open, it slammed against the doorstop as I stood at the threshold. Alison was hidden underneath the muscular bulk of the man on top of her, his hips snapping as he pounded into her.

"What the *fuck?*"

With a scream, Alison tried to sit up at my shout, her legs jerking as the man on top of her shifted.

"Who the fuck is this guy?" I shouted, slamming my palm against the door. Alison looked at me, not an ounce of remorse on her face as she rolled her eyes. *She rolled her fucking eyes at me.*

I saw red.

"Sorry, Owen, I didn't want you to find out this way." She lifted a shoulder. "He's just better than you." She threw a sly smile at the man who was now lounging comfortably in the bed next to her as though he hadn't just been caught fucking another man's woman.

That little bitch. After everything we'd done, putting everything in place to save face and using Amelia as a scapegoat, the little cunt thought she could do the same to *me?* My vision blurred, and I lunged at her, her lover coming to meet me halfway with a bang.

A bang?

Staggering backward, I clutched at the stinging

pain in my abdomen, blood running thick and fast between my fingers.

"What the fuck, Dave? You didn't have to shoot him." Alison's cry faded in and out as I stumbled backward, barely comprehending what was happening. When I hit the wall, I sank, letting my legs splay out in front of me.

Alison came into view, prying my hands away from the wound and hissing through her teeth. "Shit, he's not gonna make it. He's losing too much blood."

"Ambulance," I managed to spit out the word, along with a mouthful of blood.

Alison made a tutting sound and glanced over her shoulder at Dave. "What are we going to do?"

My gaze darted between the two of them, not understanding what was going on. Why were they trying to decide what to do? They needed to call me an ambulance. I might be able to make it through this, but they had to act quickly. My strength was wavering, and I couldn't apply enough pressure to the wound to stem the flow of blood, but neither of them were helping me.

Dave's voice echoed through the room, an inconsistent volume I could barely grasp onto. "We can get rid of the body."

Body? What body?

I was the body.

The body was me.

They were going to let me die.

Panic overtook me, and I tried to move, gritting my teeth against the pain before coughing up more blood over myself. Alison stood and stepped away from me, and I reached out to her. She looked at my outstretched hand and then turned back to Dave, saying something to him. A few words were passed back and forth, but I couldn't hear them, and I could barely see.

Then they stopped talking and simply stood there and watched me die.

With a lurch, I sat upright in bed, gasping for air and gripping my stomach.

The room was dark.

There was no pain.

Gripping my head, I took a moment to think.

I was shot.

Alison's lover boy had fucking shot me, and then...

I startled when I looked over to see Alison's

sleeping form next to me, tucked into her bundle of blankets as though nothing happened. With a roar, I grabbed the edge of the blankets and tore them from her. Alison gasped and screamed as I leaped on top of her, wrapping my fingers around her neck. "You little bitch, you tried to kill me."

Her eyes grew wide as she clawed at my fingers around her throat.

Did she think I would forget?

Did she think she could simply pretend nothing happened, and we could continue?

As her hand slapped out to the bedside table, groping for something, I followed the movement and saw the clock—*September 19, 5:15 a.m.*

Wrenching myself from Alison and off the bed, she gasped for air, rubbing her neck. "What the fuck, Owen?"

September 19.

It was not *possible.*

When I said nothing, she approached me, wrapping her arms cautiously around my middle and pressing her cheek against my back. "Talk to me, baby. What's wrong? Are you okay?"

I ran a hand through my hair, panic surging through me again at the action, but when I looked at my hand this time, there was nothing. No loose hairs. No clumps.

A dream? It must have been a dream.

But it was so raw and vivid.

I'd never had a dream like that before.

And the pain from the gunshot, the feel of my blood seeping through my fingers, was so real. You weren't supposed to feel pain in dreams. I looked down to where Alison's fingers intertwined over my stomach. No wound. No scars.

A dream.

Unwrapping her arms from me, I turned, letting her hug me again and look into my eyes. Tracing a thumb over her neck, I sighed when she flinched slightly. "I'm sorry. It was a bad dream. Did I hurt you?"

"Must have been a hell of a dream." Alison rubbed her neck. "I think I'm okay. You scared me more than hurt me." She looked up at me again and giggled. "What's up with your hair?"

"What?" I gripped it again. Were there bald patches? "What's wrong?"

She reached up and patted down my hair. "It's all sticking up at odd angles... you've got some serious bedhead." Alison tilted her head toward the en suite. "Go have a shower and get ready for work. I'm going back to bed."

Absentmindedly, I nodded.

A dream.

All a dream.

Before I left the house, I'd checked my cell. No message from Amelia's sister or anything else that had anything to do with Amelia. *Nothing.*

My hair was fine, and the drive to work was uneventful. I tried to remember any details from driving to work yesterday, anything that gave me déjà vu, but there was nothing specific from the trip I could compare to today's drive.

Of course, there wasn't—it was just *a dream.*

Already on edge when I stepped into the hospital, it didn't help that everyone was staring at me as I moved through the halls to my office. *Every single person* I passed stopped to stare at me, mouth hanging open as they gawked, eyes wide but otherwise expressionless—patients, nurses, and other doctors, *everyone.*

My nerves were frayed beyond control when I passed the administration desk on the third floor, and I spun on my heel and snapped out, "What! What are you all looking at?"

Chatter ceased, and the room fell silent aside from the consistent background staccato beeps and long whines of machines. Eyes drew to me at my outburst, and I felt the heat running up the back of my neck.

One of the administrators cleared her throat and offered meekly, "No one was looking at you, Doctor."

My eyes twitched, and without another word, I spun around and made it to my office, slamming the door behind me. Too agitated to sit still, I paced the floor, back and forth, wearing into the already worn carpet. When there was a knock at the door, I grunted.

Andrew let himself in, smirking as he followed my movements. "Bit tense there, Owen? What happened out there? Nurses told me about your little outburst."

I stopped pacing and stared at Andrew. "I don't know. I..." What could I tell him? I was losing my mind? I had a dream that was so vivid I would've sworn up and down it was real? "I didn't sleep well."

He chuckled. "Maybe Miss Alison can help you with that. I hear she helps Dave get to sleep every other night."

When I rounded on Andrew, he held his hands

up in surrender. "What the fuck did you say?"

His smile dropped. "I said maybe Miss Alison can help you with that. As in, maybe she can help you relax. Jesus, Owen, when did you become such a prude?"

"No. What did you say about Dave?"

"Who the fuck is Dave?"

We stared at each other for a beat longer, and Andrew's brows creased together. "Are you okay, man? You're freaking me out."

"I'm fine. I'm fine. Just... tired."

Andrew nodded, although his gaze told me he didn't believe me as he backed out of my office.

CHAPTER 13

OWEN

Barely making it through my shift without losing my mind, I was thankful for the end of the day. I began questioning everything everyone said and did. Several more times throughout the day, people made comments about Amelia, Alison, my cheating, or lies, and every time I asked them what the fuck they meant by that, it was like they never said it in the first place.

Andrew had grabbed my hands when I reached up and gripped his coat during lunch, practically shaking him for saying Amelia had proof I had cheated first and set the whole thing up. How would he even know anything of the sort? When I snapped, he laughed awkwardly while prying my fingers from his lapels, saying next time he won't ask if I want diet or regular soda and just get me regular if it offends me so much.

What the fuck was happening to me?

Arriving home, I kicked off my shoes and closed the door behind me before leaning against it and taking a few steadying breaths. Music was playing from upstairs, and I stilled, listening for sounds of voices or fucking. But there was none, only Alison humming along to her terrible music, probably while she did yoga or some shit.

Scowling, I moved upstairs, shouting, "Hello," to Alison before locking myself in the bathroom.

I stared at the mirror, running my hands through my hair for the thousandth time, checking for bald patches that weren't there. When I turned on the faucet to splash some water on my face, like the simple motion would clear everything up, the walls began to shake, and I gripped the sink.

The shaking didn't stop, instead intensifying, the light flickering and eventually going out as the entire room quaked. Everything on the vanity fell, and several perfume bottles smashed against the floor.

I gripped the sink, unsure what to do. *Do I get in the bathtub or the doorway?* I'd never experienced an earthquake before, and my reactions were delayed by too many false alarms throughout the day and a dream that haunted me because I still wasn't convinced it was only a dream. When I glanced in the mirror, there was an image of a man behind me, and I choked on my gasp—long, ghostly silver hair, red horns, and eyes that glowed orange.

Not a man. *The Devil.*

I cried out, turning to find no one there, and with the ground still shaking, I stumbled, stepping on broken glass and hissing through my teeth as shards embedded in my feet before I tripped and collapsed into the bath, knocking my head against the tiles.

The shaking stopped as abruptly as it started.

"Owen?" Alison's voice was followed shortly by her footsteps. She rattled against the door handle, and when it wouldn't open, she called out, "Owen, are you okay? Talk to me!"

I grumbled, rubbing my head and grunting when my fingers came away bloody. The quaking had stopped, the lights were back on, and I moved to unlock the bathroom door, walking on my heels to avoid pressing the glass farther into my feet.

But my feet weren't bleeding.

I was staring at my feet when Alison flew into the

room, reaching up and grabbing my face. "Are you okay? I heard you cry out."

I snatched a towel from next to the vanity and held it on the back of my head. "Yeah, I'm okay... just knocked my head when I tripped over after the earthquake."

Alison frowned. "Earthquake?"

"Yeah, I just..." I trailed off, glancing behind me. All the broken bottles and spilled containers were back in their place like nothing had ever happened.

"Owen, you're beginning to frighten me." She passed her hand over my forehead. "Maybe you shouldn't go to work tomorrow. You're stressed."

I nodded and kept nodding in agreement when Alison said she was going to call in sick for me tomorrow.

But I wasn't stressed.

Something else was going on.

And the only explanation that made sense was I was losing my mind.

The next morning, I woke, staring at the ceiling, knowing I didn't have to go to work. Alison said last night she had a relaxing day planned for us, whatever that meant.

Squirming under the blankets, I felt uncomfortable.

More than uncomfortable—there was pain.

There were shapes moving under the sheets, and when a sharp pain radiated from my crotch, I yelped and whipped the blankets off me.

Alison looked up at me and smiled, wedged between my legs.

Her teeth were covered in blood.

"Alison, what are you—"

She simply grinned and lifted the knife, gripping my cock with one hand and using the knife to cut it at the base with the other. I couldn't make her stop and screamed as she sawed slowly through the muscle, laughing as I tried to dislodge her grip. My hands shook as my vision started to fade, and I clung to consciousness. I didn't want to pass out, not now. Who knows what would happen while I was unconscious?

When I tried to push at her face, she bit my hand, digging through the delicate part between my thumb and forefinger and shaking her head from side to side like a dog, dislodging a chunk of flesh. My cry choked in my throat as she finished cutting, and I screamed as she removed my severed cock, blood splashing over us as she kissed the wound and then licked her lips seductively.

Tears streamed down my cheeks, and I kicked out at her weakly, but Alison ignored my struggles, instead mounting me and holding my arms by my sides between her legs.

"Alison..." I whimpered, not understanding why she would do this. The pain radiated through my body, a throb starting at the stump where my cock used to be and vibrating upward, making me want to vomit. The bed was growing wet with blood, the puddle cooling as it spread.

She leaned forward for a kiss, smearing my blood over my lips and face. When I opened my mouth to gag, she shoved my severed cock down my throat. I threw up, the vomit having nowhere to go, some of it pushed out my nostrils, and the remainder burned my throat as I struggled to breathe, panicking as I began to run out of oxygen.

Alison sat atop me, laughing as I choked to death.

I woke, staring at the ceiling.

It was dark.

Lifting the blanket, there was no pain, no blood,

and a quick reach down told me my cock was exactly where it should be.

Alison lay next to me, sleeping soundly in her bundle of blankets.

I glanced to my side at the alarm clock—*September 19, 5:15 a.m.*

Rolling over, I vomited on the floor.

CHAPTER
14

AMELIA

Unsure as to what woke me, I squirmed against the mattress. The first sound to hit my ears was my own mumble, and I tried to claw my way to the world of the waking.

How much of yesterday was a dream?

Squeezing my eyes shut, I tried to force myself further awake. It was a herculean effort, like I was drugged, drowsiness trying to lure me back to sleep.

Why was I awake?

Blinking rapidly, it was still dark.

"What time is it?" I muttered more to myself than to anyone. I didn't expect Draven back so soon, and I almost laughed at the idea I was waiting for a demon to come home to me. When I tried to roll over, I realized my hands were bound above my head, tied tight against the headboard. The ache in my arms startled me when I yanked against them, and I stopped struggling immediately. Now wide awake, I stared around the room. "Draven?" I whispered into the darkness.

He appeared in a wisp of pale gray smoke, and I had to blink again to make sure I hadn't imagined the strange entrance. "You're awake, kitten."

"What time is it? Why am I tied up? What's going on?"

The mattress creaked under his weight as he kneeled on the side of the bed, crawling over to me. I didn't shrink away from him but also denied myself the need to reach for him or arch my back against his warmth as his body came over mine. I'd woken tied up, and it was disorientating.

"It's eight o'clock."

My brows furrowed as that didn't make any sense. "Are you saying I slept for almost twenty hours?"

Draven pouted, mischief playing across his eyes. "My poor kitten must've been tired."

"What aren't you telling me?" He laughed as I glared at him.

"Maybe I helped you sleep."

"You drugged me?" The idea shocked me, and I recoiled back into the pillows this time, trying to put distance between his body and mine. "Why would you do that?" It seemed such an invasive thing and entirely unnecessary. I'd given myself to him, promised myself to him, and after we had sex, he still felt the need to drug me.

Draven chuckled again, a low rumble that reverberated deep through his chest. He traced a finger down my cheek, smirking as I twisted my head away from his touch. "I didn't need to drug you. I simply made you sleep."

I had no idea what powers this demon held, and the thought tugged at my chest when I realized I didn't want to be controlled by him. I didn't *need* to be controlled. I'd submitted willingly. "Don't you trust me not to run?"

He tilted his head. "You needed rest."

"But why am I tied up?" He apparently was content ignoring that until I brought it to his attention, and when his gaze traced up my body to where my wrists were bound against the headboard, his eyes glowed brighter, and I shuddered at the desire in his face.

"That's for the fun we're about to have."

Shifting, he ripped the blanket from me and took a moment to take in my naked body with his hungry gaze before gently scratching his claws over my skin from my neck and working down. I couldn't stop from arching against his touch. I was already aching for him. "Wh-what about Owen?"

He laughed loud this time, throwing his head back before coming to me, hovering his lips over mine, barely a whisper away. "So hungry for revenge… I thought you'd be hungry for me instead?"

"I am, *I am*. Pleas—" Draven slapped his hand over my mouth, drawing his hand away, and ended by dragging his fingers over my lips, his eyebrow arched in amusement.

"I haven't finished with Owen yet, but I couldn't stay away from you. I thought we'd have a celebratory fuck, then I'll be away again. The wheels are in motion, and that disease of a man is already suffering."

"How?" I asked, managing to stop myself from stuttering. A hunger grew in my gut at the idea of Owen finally paying for his sins against me. I wanted to know what was happening, what he was *feeling,* and if he knew yet what it was like to lose every damn thing.

Tearing my eyes away from Draven's, I frowned.

He was right—I was hungry for revenge, *desperate* for it.

Was this all that consumed me now?

And once I'd had my revenge, once Draven had made Owen suffer, what was left of me then?

Draven traced a claw down the side of my face, his hand moving to clamp over my mouth again. "So many thoughts going on in that pretty head. Why don't you just stop thinking for a while?"

I tried asking a question, one of the many floating around in my mind, but the one pushing hardest for an answer flickered forward, *When this is all over, what happens to me?*

Draven tutted, smirking again. "Weren't you listening earlier, kitten? When this is over, you're mine. You can stay here and live out whatever life you choose, or you can come back with me. Either way, you'll spend most of your time with my cock inside you."

I shuddered at the boldness of his words, whipping through scenarios of all the things I'd like him to do to me. Were there to be no consequences for me summoning Draven in the first place? A lifetime of sex didn't seem like a punishment. His smile widened as he watched me. How much of my thoughts could he read? Or was it just a feeling? I'd ask him one day if he'd let me.

"I'm not much the domestic type, but I'd understand if you'd rather stay on Earth." He seemed to be mulling over the possibilities as he spoke aloud, "But there's plenty of time to sort that later. You're interrupting my playtime."

When I started muffling out another question against his warm fingers, Draven hushed me gently, removing his hand to brush his lips against mine in a lover's caress. "*How* I'm torturing Owen is not for you to know, my dear. Now make yourself comfortable. You're going to be here for a while."

"Draven—"

He ceased the gentle scratching of his claws down my body and stared at me, his eyes darkening. "If you're going to keep asking questions, Amelia..." letting his voice trail off, he looked at me thoughtfully for another moment before gracefully lifting himself off the bed and moving to the en suite. When he returned with a pair of my underwear, I yanked on the binds holding me to the bed.

"Did you get those from the laundry basket?"

With a devilish grin, he lifted them to his nose and inhaled deeply. "I had to. You weren't wearing any I could take off and shove in your mouth."

"In my mou—" I choked out a gasp as he shoved the bundled-up cotton past my lips, pushing in and around my mouth with his fingers. When I mumbled out a protest, he drew a rope from the air, weaving it around his fingers as he pulled it from nothingness before tying it around my head, holding the gag in place.

"There will be plenty of time for questions later, my kitten, but I came back to satiate my own desires. Is that understood?"

I nodded, and he chuckled as he kneeled next to me again, drifting a hand lazily down my body before cupping my pussy in his palm and pressing a finger inside me. I arched against him, but it wasn't enough, and even as he curled his finger inside me, pressing against my walls and making me moan, I still wanted more.

"You need to learn not to question me, kitten, so I'm afraid I need to discipline you." His words and tone were apologetic, but the flaring of lust in his gaze told me he wasn't sorry at all. Before I could question, there were more ropes and knots until my legs were tied at the ankles, held open and bound to the corners of the bed frame, spread-eagle with nowhere to hide.

I shuddered as he crawled over me, coming to rest between my legs and pressing his hands against my thighs. His tongue swiped up my pussy, and I bucked against his face, moaning into the gag when he did it again. With playful licks and nips, Draven worked me expertly toward my peak, and I was squirming under his touch, ready to cry out as I came.

Then he stopped.

With a groan, I dropped my hips back onto the mattress, eyeing Draven desperately as he gazed down at me, his face slick with my juices. The orgasm that had been so close ebbed away, and my clit throbbed harder with the denial. I glared at him, but before I could try to speak, he was between my legs again, this time curling two fingers inside me as his tongue worked against my clit, intermittently sucking it hard. The pleasure threatened to peak faster this time, and I panted and squirmed, ready for release.

Draven stopped again.

As I cried out in frustration, he simply chuckled and scratched delicately along the inside of my thighs. "Shh, kitten, we're only just starting."

He brought me to the edge of my peak and pulled away before release four more times. Each time, I chased his mouth and fingers with my hips, lifting toward him and desperate for the final touch that would send me over the edge. Each time he denied me, and by the third time, tears were leaking down the sides of my face.

"Please," I cried out against the gag, the word coming out only as a muffled sound.

I moaned as Draven kneeled between my legs, pumping his cock in his palm. My body was trembling, and when he swiped the head of his cock over my oversensitive clit, I screamed, trying to pull away from the overloading sensation. With a single thrust forward, he was fully seated inside me, snarling as my back arched off the bed at his intrusion and pleasure. He began thrusting hard, and I had to wind my hands around the ropes binding my wrists, trying to anchor myself still as the demon pounded relentlessly into me.

"Amelia…"

Draven's voice was dangerously sweet, honey-laced with poison as I opened my eyes and dragged my gaze to his, trying to mumble something around my gag but unsure of what I wanted to say. My body was limp as he gripped my hips, lifting the bottom half of my body off the bed for better access. He removed one hand from my hip and repositioned it, hovering his thumb and forefinger over my clit. My eyes widened as I followed his movement, and with a harsh pinch on my clit, I fell apart as he commanded me, "*Come.*"

All the pleasure he'd denied me came at once, and I screamed around the gag, arching until my wrists and ankles pulled painfully against the restraints. Draven drove into me harder and faster, his claws drawing blood on my hips until, with another snarl, he came, the warmth from his release dripping from me as he pulled out.

The ropes around my hands, wrists, and head unwound themselves, disappearing back into the air as though they were never there. Tentatively and with a groan, I lowered my arms, and Draven crawled over me, pulling the saliva-soaked panties from my mouth and tracing his tongue along my lips as I moaned.

"Rest now, Amelia," he whispered against my skin. "I'll be back. Now *sleep.*"

My eyes shot open at his final words, that dark shadow passing across them, the same tone he uses when he makes me come with his words alone. He was sending me to sleep, drugging me with his power.

"Wait..." But sleep had already taken over, and as

I fought against it, my eyes drooped closed, Draven's smirk the last thing I saw before sleep took me again.

15

OWEN

September 19, 5:15 a.m.
September 19, 5:15 a.m.
September 19, 5:15 a.m.

I was definitely losing my mind.

Sometimes I'd live out the day, hallucinating the entire time.

People would say and do things in my mind that were so real, but when I followed up with them or other witnesses present, no one else saw what I saw.

I'd go to bed and wake up the next day.

Only it wasn't the next day—it was the nineteenth over and over again.

Every day one of my nightmares came true. My lies were exposed. Alison left me for someone younger than me, richer and better looking. There were days I couldn't get Amelia out of my head, and I pined for her, once even going to her house only to find her in the arms of another man, younger than me, better than me, making her come. One time, it was several men, and she was pinned between them, her eyes flashing with pleasure at my pain as she was fucked in every hole, and I stood there watching, unable to look away.

Then it would be the nineteenth again.

Twice I'd lost my job. Once because my lies were exposed, and I never even found out what evidence was had against me so I could try to remember to tie off the loose end. Once because I'd snapped after another vision and attacked a patient, sure he was the devil I'd seen standing behind me in mirrors and next to me in window reflections every day. He was always smiling, his eyes glowing. The Devil was tormenting me. I could feel it. The idea didn't help because it only made me sound crazier.

There was no one I could talk to.

I tried talking to Alison a few times. Sometimes she'd leave me, and other times she'd attack me. I gave up trying to ask for help.

September 19, 5:15 a.m.

Several times I'd died.

Always in bloody, painful, and horrific manners.

The pain was too visceral for it to be a dream. So I must be losing my mind.

You don't feel pain in dreams—everyone knows that. But I remembered what it felt like to get shot, to have my cock severed from my body, to be beaten to death with a brick, to have my eyes clawed out by manicured fingernails, and to be hit by a train.

Today, I woke, and it was the same—*September 19, 5:15 a.m.*

God help me.

September 19, 11:59 p.m.

I'd done this before, waited until past midnight until I could no longer keep my eyes open.

I'd stayed awake for more than twenty-four hours in the past, but I could never manage it this time. Sleep would always lure me into its depths before three in the morning, and I'd always wake up, and it would be the nineteenth again.

Today, I did nothing.

I didn't get out of bed or make a call to tell the hospital I wouldn't be in. I let Alison do that when she went to pick up a shift after another administration staff member's car broke down. I stayed in bed, staring at the clock.

Alison returned, I ate nothing for dinner, and she was worried. She climbed into bed behind me, rubbing my shoulders and talking to me gently. I had no idea what she was saying, unable to bring myself to listen.

I lasted until two in the morning.

When I woke, I stared at the ceiling, wondering if there was any respite from this hell. Slowly, I turned my head, already prepared to see the same thing—*September 20, 7:00 a.m.*

I sat bolt upright, making Alison moan and roll over as I grabbed the clock from the bedside table, double and triple-checking.

The *twentieth*.

The nightmare was over.

Sighing loudly, I slid back down in the bed, and Alison moaned and stretched as she woke. Rolling to face me, she draped an arm across my chest. "How are you feeling, baby?" Her eyes rounded as she looked up at me, resting her chin on my chest.

"You look a lot better. I was so worried about you yesterday."

Keeping my voice as even as possible, I even attempted a smile. "I'm okay, just felt like hell yesterday." I repressed a shudder. No one ever needed to know about what I'd experienced. I'd be called crazy and lose everything for real if anyone thought I genuinely believed what I'd been through was real. If it was truly over, it was best to shut it behind closed doors and never let it see the light of day again. "Are you rostered on today?"

Wiping her eyes with the back of her hand, Alison shook her head. "Nope, and you're not either. I double-checked yesterday." She brightened as she looked at me again. "Want to have a relaxing day together? We could go to a spa, maybe a winery—"

Terror took over at the idea of leaving the house, where anything could happen. Sitting up, I grabbed her hands and smiled when she started looking worried again, putting her at ease. "How about we stay home together instead?" When she pouted, I brushed my thumb along her lip. "That way, we don't have to get dressed."

Alison's frown was replaced with a sultry look as she dropped a shoulder and tilted her head at me, her lips parting as she straddled me. Without another word, she was already guiding my cock inside her, and I sighed, leaning back and letting her ride me.

All the while trying to shake the feeling this normality couldn't last and was simply another illusion.

Would I ever trust reality again?

16

DRAVEN

Now it was simply a matter of waiting for the right moment. I'd already tested myself with Alison, and as suspected, she would be easy to possess—little substance and even less fight in her. I slipped in and out of her body briefly to check, and there was no resistance.

This was going to be fun.

Owen was at breaking point after having relived the past day in all its variations a hundred and seventeen times. It was obvious he was trying his best to relax, but he was always on edge, scared he was going to go back to sleep and wake up to find it was the nineteenth again or the twentieth. For all he knew, he was destined to live out every horrific version of every day for the rest of his years.

But that's not what I had planned for him, and I didn't have time to babysit him through his visions every day. So I let him wake up to a new day with a fresh bout of hope and a healthy dose of uncertainty.

How does it feel not to know when your world is going to fall apart again?

When Alison suggested they take a bath together, it was my moment—my final curtain call before I could return to Amelia and have her forever. Sliding across the room in the shadows, I moved into Alison's body, taking a moment to make sure she *knew* she was being possessed until I could feel her fear burning inside as I moved her body around as though it were my own.

"Do you want a glass of wine, babe?" I said, my voice coming out as Alison's from her body, while Alison's mind screamed behind me, attempting to warn Owen about dangers she didn't yet understand.

Owen turned to face me, his mind ticking over before he nodded. "Sure, thank you."

Smiling, I grabbed Alison's robe and shrugged it onto her body before leaving the room and skipping down the stairs while humming.

Internally, I whispered to Alison, *You have a nice body. I could do so many fun things with it.*

Her response was panicked and echoing as she struggled against the possession, but it was too late now. I had already taken hold. The time to fight would be when you first felt the darkness enter your heart, but she was used to holding darkness there and not caring for others beyond her own personal gain. She didn't notice my presence until it was too late.

Striding over to the kitchen drawers, swaying Alison's hips more than required, I reached in and sought out a large knife. Alison's fingers seized and hesitated before I could wrap them around the handle, and I stilled.

She was fighting the possession.

There must be good left in her.

I forced past her resistance and grabbed the knife, holding the blade against Alison's throat and hearing her voice whimper internally. Speaking out loud, the words sounded in her voice. "I could do anything right now, Alison. I could make you slit your own throat or maybe your wrists, make it look like you couldn't take Owen's lies anymore."

Her voice echoed in my mind, *Is this about Amelia?*

A surge of rage pumped through me that she'd even *dared* to say Amelia's name, and Alison's mind shrank away from the feeling of anger that surrounded her. I stood in front of the oven, making sure she could see her reflection through her eyes as I smiled with her pretty mouth, offering her a single nod.

Before I showed her Hell.

A split second was all it took—images of burning flesh in hellfire and tortured souls desperate to escape eternity.

Who are you? Her internal cry was desperate.

Chuckling, the sound coming from her lips as her sweet giggle, I answered her internally, *You can call me* Judgment.

I ignored the rest of her screams as she watched from behind her eyes while I slid the knife into the pocket of her robe. Her scream reverberated through my mind, and I had to clamp Alison's jaw to stop the sound from working its way up her throat. In her panic, she was fighting the possession, gripping hold of a conscience and guilt she had lingering within.

Alison wasn't innocent, but she wasn't as guilty as Owen.

I could feel it within her.

She didn't deserve the same fate he did.

Change of plan.

Tilting forward, I ran head-first into the wall, slipping from Alison's body as her head collided with the plaster, and she dropped to the floor unconscious. I watched her breathing for a moment before sliding her robe from her and shrugging it on myself, the fabric stretching around my arms. Snatching the wine bottle and glasses and moving up the stairs when I burst into the bathroom, Owen was already sinking into the warm water, the scents of oils and bath salts thick in the air. He smiled lazily as his head lolled to the side, nodding at me and seeing only what I wanted him to see—Alison's body—before closing his eyes as I motioned with the glass and poured him some chilled sparkling wine.

Placing the glasses and bottle on the edge of the spa bath, I shrugged out of Alison's robe, leaving it and the knife by the side of the large tub.

Stepping into the water, I hummed appreciatively at its warmth and immediately sidled up to Owen, draping my knees over his and interlocking our legs. He made a sound of appreciation as I reached into the water and started stroking his cock, working hands that looked to him like Alison's over the organ. Owen moaned and tilted his head back against the tiles, his jaw slack and eyes closed peacefully. "Babe, you know just how to make me feel better."

I chuckled. "Just relax and let me take care of you, baby."

Owen nodded, keeping his head tilted back, and let me caress his cock with slow, gentle strokes, not with the intention of getting him off, just a relaxing and delicate touch. Reaching down, I cupped his balls, rolling them around my palms.

Quietly, I slid the knife under the water, tucking it under my leg.

"Do you want to have kids one day, babe?"

His eyes shot open, looking at me and searching Alison's face as I rearranged my expression into a blank smile. "Yeah, I'd love that."

"Me too." I giggled, and with a smile, Owen closed his eyes again, resting his head back and relaxing further into the water. "Does that feel good, baby?"

"So good, Alison…" he murmured.

"It's a shame we haven't had kids yet," I sighed out the words, and he simply hummed again, not really paying attention under the ministrations of my fingers around his balls.

"Why's that?" he asked dreamily.

"Because you have no balls, babe."

There was a *snick* sound as I sliced into his sack, and the water flooded with red a split second before the pain hit Owen. His brow furrowed, "Careful, Alison, that hurts." I smirked, gripping his balls hard and yanking them down so I could cut through the rest of the skin in one move. Owen screamed, launching himself to his feet and spraying my face with blood as I held his balls in my hand.

I laughed, the sound coming out high-pitched and maniacal, a combination of Alison's voice and my own, a sound that would haunt him forever.

Owen was still screaming, the sound reaching a new volume, when I stepped out of the bathtub and flushed his balls down the toilet. His eyes went wide and manic, and he grabbed a towel and clutched it between his legs, screaming and writhing as he sunk to the floor. I crouched next to him, dropping the bloodied knife by his side as I revealed my true form, my silver hair wet at the ends from sitting in the bathtub and sticking to my warm skin. Owen screamed louder. He'd seen me throughout his torture, appearing in mirrors and window reflections, looking at him out of the shadows, and driving him crazier with each passing repetition of the day he suffered through over and over.

I gripped his hair, yanking his head up until his face was level with mine, tears streaming down his flushed cheeks. "You should consider yourself lucky, Owen," I snarled out the words, letting them drip with the darkness that ran through my veins. He couldn't respond, whimpering and sniffling as he clutched the towel to the open wound between his legs. "This is your punishment for what you did to Amelia. One less thing you'll be tortured for in Hell."

Alison stumbled into the room, crying out when she saw me, naked and crouching over Owen and the blood painted across the bathroom tiles—a color they'd never be able to get out. No amount of washing would remove that from their memories.

"Call a fucking ambulance!" Owen cried, and there was the barest second of hesitation and fear in her eyes when she caught my gaze before Alison ran to the bedroom to grab her cell.

Tomorrow Owen would wake in a hospital bed, handcuffed to the side and awaiting a psych evaluation. Fingerprints on the knife and the angle of the cut would show he severed his own scrotum, and his pleas would fall on deaf ears.

The Devil made me do it.

Alison knew the truth, but she harbored enough

self-preservation to know if she stood in solidarity with Owen, she would go down with him, being called out as being as crazy as he was. So she'd offer her support, but only silently, and eventually, she'd drift away, unable to take the reality and reminder of the hell she witnessed because of him.

She'll turn her life around and become a better person. She had that ability inside her.

It would be the twenty-first tomorrow. A dark new reality for Owen and the first day of the rest of his life.

And he would wish today had been an illusion too.

CHAPTER
17

AMELIA

Once again, dragging myself from sleep was a chore, and I grumbled, rolling over and grabbing a handful of blankets, taking them with me. A dark chuckle emanated from somewhere above me, and I stilled, my breath coming out in short bursts and between my legs already slickening with arousal.

Draven was back.

His voice did unspeakable things to me. He didn't even need to touch me or say anything particularly dirty before I was dripping wet for him. There was a deep inhale of breath and another chuckle.

"Having sweet dreams about me, kitten?"

I whimpered, rubbing my legs together.

Draven gripped the blankets and ripped them

from me, and I rolled onto my back to find him kneeling at my feet, cock erect and dripping with precum.

Licking my lips, I eyed his cock before meeting his burning gaze. "Um, Draven..." It was difficult to concentrate as he started moving toward me, straddling my body so his cock hovered over my breasts. "I, uh... haven't eaten in a few days, I'm guessing." I paused to throw a glare at him. Time had no meaning when you were being lulled into an enchanted sleep. "And I really need a shower and something to drink too."

Draven eyed me, apparently considering my words. "I guess I forgot you're only human." He shifted, and I sighed, thinking he was about to move off me. Instead, he moved forward again, pinning my arms to my sides with his legs and positioning until his cock was over my face. "You can eat, drink, and bathe soon, kitten, but the revenge is complete, and right now, I need that sweet mouth of yours."

I couldn't keep my eyes on his face, despite the sculptured features I'd only read about in romance books—an exaggerated version of everything attractive to me. The slight red tinge to his skin was enhanced by the wetness on the tip of his cock, and languidly he began pumping his cock in his hand, watching my eyes. Sure, I'd gone down on Owen before, but I doubt I was capable of the sort of lurid experience Draven would expect. When I finally raised my eyes to his, he was smiling, a lazy, casual smile that relaxed me but only a bit.

"You're worried you won't please me." It was a statement, but I nodded anyway. Draven had brought nothing but pleasure to my body, and I wanted to do the same for him. If for nothing else but to say thank you for another chance at life and because I wanted to know what he tasted like. "You'll learn soon enough, kitten."

With that, he leaned forward, planting his fists on either side of my head and tilting his hips so his cock was pressing against my lips. Obediently, I parted my lips, and with a liquid-smooth motion, he thrust into my waiting mouth. Draven groaned, and his fingers gripped my hair. A flush of wetness soaked my thighs at the sounds he made as he thrust past my lips. Animalistic growls and grunts accompanied his use of my mouth. I tried to create a rhythm with his movements, flicking my tongue around the head as he pulled back and sucking when he was deep in my throat.

"Amelia..." He snarled, twisting his clawed fingers through my hair. "That's it, that's what I fucking need."

I couldn't move, trapped between his legs, and could only allow him to use me as he pleased. Rubbing my thighs together, I needed something, *any* friction I could get to ease the ache created purely by Draven being near me. When my jaw began to ache, I didn't complain, and Draven changed angles, driving into my mouth hard and fast. My breathing became ragged, trying to time my breaths between his thrusts as his movements became sporadic.

With a painful yank of my hair, he commanded, "Swallow." His cock was so deep in my throat I wouldn't have had a choice even if he had said nothing. Draven's cum pumped down my throat, and I accepted the salty tang gratefully.

Draven rolled off me, waving his hand in the direction of the en suite. "Go have a shower, then we'll eat." I shifted to the edge of the mattress, my legs weak underneath me. Draven lay silently as I stumbled from one piece of furniture to another, unaware I'd be so weak from so long in bed without food or water. Unable to hold myself up any longer, I almost collapsed, landing in his arms instead of on the floor as he chuckled again.

Throwing me over his shoulder, I squealed as he

moved toward the en suite, and I managed to shoo him away to allow me a moment of privacy to use the bathroom. When he returned, he turned on the faucets to run a bath before laying me down against the cool tiles of the tub as it finished filling.

"Stay here." He disappeared out the door, and I sank against the curve of the bathtub, letting the water soothe me.

Minutes later, Draven returned with a glass and a jug of cool water, pouring me some and helping me take small sips. There was a crumpling as he opened a bag of crisps and offered it to me, and I hummed as I took a handful, shoving them unceremoniously in my mouth before taking more.

Draven turned off the taps, grabbed a washcloth and soap, and began washing my body, starting with my legs and massaging my feet as I polished off the bag of crisps, forgetting until I was finished to offer him some and feeling the heat rise in my cheeks. "I'm sorry, Amelia," he said as he moved to wash my back, encouraging me to sit forward. "I didn't take care of you well enough."

"You were busy."

He laughed, a low rumble moving through his chest, his hands feeling warm on my skin even compared to the heat of the water. "I'll remember to let you eat and drink in the future."

I couldn't help the laugh that escaped at the absurdity of the statement. "Thank you."

Draven smiled as he finished washing me before he lifted my body from the tub and stood me, guiding my hands to rest on his shoulders as he kneeled to dry me off. As he worked, I twisted a few strands of his long, silver hair between my fingers, taking the chance to explore him as he had done me. When he made no complaints, I moved my hands around and touched the horns where they protruded from his upper forehead. They too were warm to the touch, and I followed the twisted pattern around the horns before gripping them with both hands when he pressed his mouth to my stomach, sucking the skin. "Careful, Amelia..." he warned, nipping at my flesh.

"W-why?"

"That's a sensitive spot where you have your hands."

Eyes widening, I glanced down at where I gripped his horns, and feeling bold, instead of releasing them, I ran my hands up and down as I would his cock. Draven groaned, and his teeth sank into my hip, making me cry out and release his horns from my grip.

"Noted," I said, feeling breathless at the intensity of his reaction to my touch. "Do you want me to order us a pizza?"

His gaze raised to mine, this demon on his knees before me, worshiping my body as he had said he would. "Would that make you happy?"

"Yes." My voice was small. I owed him. I was in debt to Draven, not the other way around. How could a demon be the one to care about my happiness?

He smirked once again as though he could read my thoughts. "Then that's what we'll do."

I nodded, unable to stop the thoughts racing through my mind even as I moved away to grab my cell to order, shrugging on a robe.

This was an incredibly bizarre situation, and I didn't know what to think, but one thought was at the forefront of my mind, and I couldn't get around it.

What happens now?

18

DRAVEN

Amelia hadn't asked again about the revenge I took on Owen, not that I'd given her much of a chance. I watched her now as she happily munched on pizza, sipped a soft drink, and chuckled at some comedy film she'd chosen from a streaming service. She did look brighter now she'd had something to eat and drink, was clean, and looked almost... relaxed.

Relaxed in *my* presence as though I wasn't a demon she had sold her soul and body to in exchange for teaching a bad man some much-needed lessons.

Maybe she simply wasn't facing the reality of the situation yet. My brow furrowed. This troubled me. Glancing at her, Amelia smiled and handed me a slice of pizza, and I almost burst out laughing. Instead, I chuckled again and accepted the offer. She was an innocent soul. I felt that when she called me, knowing it was part of what drew me to her—an innocent soul tainted and marked by the need for revenge and by the scars of pain that only revenge could help smooth over but never remove.

I had to have her.

Now I had her, I would keep her.

Amelia had looked at me strangely earlier when I mentioned I wanted her to be happy. She was my kitten. Did humans not want their pets to be happy? But she was more than that—she was my body and soul to look after and keep, beyond fucking. I did care for her, a possessiveness that flared under my skin and scorched me when I thought about her too hard.

She was mine.

Had she accepted that?

When the movie was over, and Amelia was full and content, she curled up against the couch, faced and watched me over the empty pizza box between us. "What happens now?"

I watched her, smirking every time her eyes flickered away from my face to trace the lines of my body. I was still naked, always was. On the other hand, Amelia had a white robe pulled around her, cinched tightly at the waist so all I could see were her long legs curled underneath her as she studied me as much as I did her. "Do you regret what you did?" I asked. She paused for a moment, rolling the thought around in her mind as her mouth twisted and ran through the whirlwind of emotions.

"Did Owen…" Amelia trailed off, unable to say the word *suffer* out loud, lest it remind her of the part of herself that wanted him to. The part of her that only days ago wanted nothing more than revenge to the point it took over her entire being.

My fangs were exposed as I smiled. "He suffered. Longer than you can possibly know. The day you slept was an eternity for him. Then he came crashing back to reality with a permanent reminder of the pain he went through. Alison and Owen are no more, and he'll have to find the strength to go on with his life when his own sanity has been brought into question." I held Amelia's stare as her eyes widened. "He'll have to summon the strength to move forward after being broken down into nothing, just like you did."

Her lip quirked. "I only found the strength through summoning you."

I shoved the pizza box onto the floor with a

flourish and grabbed her robe, tugging her until she slid across the couch and her chest was next to mine. "No. You found the strength on your own. The power you felt surging through you during the ceremony was *you,* not me."

"You knew about that?" Amelia's voice was small.

I nodded. "I felt you. Every part of you in that moment when you called to me. We were connected before you were even sure I existed."

Amelia's brows drew together as she looked down at the couch, glancing over where my hands still gripped her robe. Her lip twitched again. It was almost a smile, and I smirked. It was enough. "I just figured you'd cut his balls off or something."

I barked out a laugh. "I did that too. Well, Alison did."

Her gaze shot to my face, eyes searching mine for a hint of a lie she wouldn't find. "You're serious, aren't you?"

"Of course."

Her lip twitched, then she giggled, and the giggle morphed into a laugh, which ended as abruptly as it started. She then slapped a hand over her mouth, eyes back on mine as she realized she was laughing at another human's suffering.

Peeling her hand away from her face, I held her wrists. "No, no, *no*. You don't get to have an attack of conscience now. He deserved punishment for what he did to you. Karma came back around in a circle."

"Isn't the idea of Karma... the same treatment comes back to you through the universe?"

"Maybe I'm acting on behalf of the universe."

Amelia chuckled. I liked the sound. I liked the way it rang against my ears and the shape of her lips when she smiled. Almost as much as I liked the sounds she made when she came. "Okay. But you still haven't answered my question. What happens now?"

"You can come back with me." The innocence of her eyes widened as her mind was filled with images of places surrounded by flames and torture fueled me. Already my fingers were tapping an impatient tune against her wrists, willing her to understand how this worked so I could get back to fucking her. I wouldn't make her sleep this time but leave her to look after herself. She'd want for nothing—not money nor possessions—Amelia would be as pleasured as I was.

"Or," I continued, growling low when she bit her lip in indecision. "You can stay here. In this town or another, I don't care. You can work and have a life of your own. But you may not take on a lover other than me, and you must be ready and willing at any time of the day or night for me to fuck you. Because you're *mine*, Amelia." I yanked her closer again, relishing in the gasp that escaped her lips. "If I want to fuck you in the middle of the day and you're at work... that's your problem, not mine."

Her mind was flooded with images of me bending her over a desk and yanking up her pencil skirt so I could fuck her hard against the cool wood, and the scent of her arousal flooded the air between us. I helped the images along, pushing her imagination further, making her *feel* my cock as though it was inside her now, and her jaw dropped as if her mouth was opening in a silent scream of pleasure.

Shifting so I could clasp her hands in one of mine, I yanked her robe open, tugging roughly at the tie and ignoring her grunts as the fabric pulled against her waist. When I touched her, her breast was heavy against my palm, my thumb grazing over the nipple that hardened into a point at my touch. This wanton side of her drew a snarl from me. She'd made a choice and agreed to give herself to me in exchange for revenge. I sensed no regret from her—

the taste of it would be bitter in the air around me. There was hesitation, of course, with visions of her mulling over what her future held when I could claim her at any moment.

I squeezed her breast, molding it in my hand. "I might come to you at night, kitten, and fuck you while you sleep so you wake up stretched around my cock with my hand clamped over your mouth. You might be shopping, and I'll drag you into a quiet corner and press you against the wall. Only you can see me, Amelia. Imagine what might happen if you're caught with your skirt around your waist, your tight little cunt exposed and dripping for the world to see."

She shuddered, even as she arched her back into my touch. "Draven… you wouldn't—"

"Wouldn't I?" The whisper was a deadly promise against her ear. When she trembled again, I chuckled. "No, I wouldn't do that. No one is to see you but me. You're *mine* and *mine* alone. If I exposed you to the world, I'd be no better than Owen, and you'd hate me for it."

Her eyes met mine—hazel, bright, and alert. When she ran her teeth over her bottom lip, I leaned forward, taking her lip in my mouth and sucking, running my fangs gently along the inside before letting go. "I may force you to the point where pain meets pleasure while I fuck you, Amelia, but I won't hurt you, not like he did."

"I believe you," she whispered.

Releasing her from my grasp, I shoved the fabric from the robe over her shoulders. "Take this off before I rip it to shreds."

CHAPTER 19

AMELIA

Hurrying to comply with Draven's demand, I stood on shaky legs, shrugging the robe off my shoulders and letting it drop to the floor. The demon before me seemed determined to break me of any modesty I had, at least around him, and was apparently willing to shred every piece of clothing I owned to rags if I tried to cover myself around him.

His hands found my breasts again as his hot breath hit my stomach, pawing and clawing at me, the sharp drag of his claws an exquisite contrast to the warmth of his hands.

"Anything I want..." Draven muttered more to himself than to me as he let his claws drag down my stomach and around my hips before cupping my ass and pulling me against him, again inhaling deeply. Spinning me around, he spread my cheeks, and my face heated as I turned to see him simply staring at me, exposed to him.

"Bend over, Amelia."

"Draven…"

I yelped when his claws dug into my flesh, claws he seemed to be able to extend and retract at will, and a growl rumbled through his chest. "Don't make me tell you again."

Swearing my face was burning red at this point, I bent at the hips, placing my hands on the coffee table in front of me. Draven traced his tongue along the crease of my cheek near my thigh, and I squirmed under his touch, yelping when he again spread my cheeks and tongued at my rear hole.

"Draven!" I jolted away from the touch, eliciting another snarl from him, once again gripping me and bringing me back to him.

His voice was a low growl, vibrating through his lips as he held me still, tracing his mouth over my skin. "Don't pull away from me again, Amelia, or I'll spank your ass until it's as red as your cheeks right now." I stilled, unable to stop myself from jerking when his tongue met my hole again, gliding around it as he hummed before pushing against the resistance.

I tensed, and he chuckled. "Relax, I'm not going to fuck your ass." He hummed again, the sound ending in a growl, and I shuddered. "Not today, anyway. I'm just exploring what's mine."

"*Yours*?" I pushed out the word with a shuddering breath. I hadn't intended it to sound like a question, and in response, Draven gripped me harder, his claws pressing painfully into my hips.

"*Mine*." There was a finality to the word, and I shuddered again, arousal blooming between my thighs. My desire for Draven hadn't ebbed or faded, only grown stronger and continued to. He'd given me my life and myself back. I could go anywhere from here. Be anyone. Nothing was holding me back, and until everything fell apart, I hadn't even realized I was bound to Owen's and everyone else's expectations.

Now the only binds I wanted to be in were Draven's as he fucked me.

He chuckled again, and I gasped. "Okay, you have to tell me, Draven... can you read my thoughts?"

"Why? Because I knew exactly when you were thinking of being fucked by me?"

My cheeks heated again, and I attempted to straighten, only for Draven to place his hand on my lower back, silently instructing me to stay bent over. "Yes," I muttered.

"Not exactly. I can't pick up on every thought like reading a book, but I get snippets. Sometimes complete thoughts but mostly incomplete. Feelings, images, senses..." I glanced back at him as the fire burned in his gaze, "... urges—"

"But—"

"We've talked enough already." Draven stood, the hard line of his erection pressing against my ass. His finger traced my hole, and I bit my lip, fighting the urge not to pull away.

"You said not today." I whimpered.

"I did. I said I wouldn't fuck your ass today." He glanced around, his gaze settling on a magazine. Leaning over to snatch it up, he folded it in half and held it in front of my face. "Bite down on this." When I opened my mouth to ask what he was doing, he shoved the magazine between my teeth, grabbing my jaw and clamping it closed. Holding my eye contact as I gazed over my shoulder, Draven dipped two fingers into his mouth, sucking and licking them slowly, teasing me with the sight. "Consider this your first lesson."

I mumbled against the magazine, drool already leaking out the sides of my mouth as he held one cheek open and poised two fingers at the entrance to my ass. His smile was dark and deadly, and I trembled, clenching and unclenching, trying to prepare myself for what was to come.

"You're *mine*, Amelia," he crooned before he shoved both fingers into my ass to the knuckle. I cried out, my teeth clamping down against the shiny magazine cover, as my body fought against the intrusion. Even when there was pain as he started pumping his fingers in and out of me, I couldn't help rocking my hips against him, wetness leaking down my legs. Draven used me thoroughly and completely, and when he bent over and whispered against my ear, never letting up on his fingers thrusting, I shuddered, "Are you ready, kitten?"

Ready? I mumbled something incoherent around the magazine.

His eyes blackened, the fiery pits of his pupils opening up and claiming me, sucking me into their depths as he licked his lips. "*Come.*"

My back arched as the orgasm hit, and I clenched around his fingers as he stilled them, holding my hips and letting me ride through the pleasure of my release. Panting, the magazine dropped to the coffee table, and I cried out when he removed his fingers and reached down to pump his cock a few times before lining it up with my pussy. He said nothing and pushed inside in one smooth motion, ending with a harsh thrust that had me jolting forward. With a kick, he sent the coffee table flying, and I flinched at the sound of it tumbling over and hitting the television cabinet. I dropped my hands to the carpet, trying to brace myself, and Draven reached around to grab my thighs, lifting my feet off the floor.

"What are you doing?" I cried out.

Draven was strong, and I didn't feel insecure in his grip, but my hands were almost lifted off the floor with every thrust, my legs stretched open to accommodate him. Again, he didn't answer but continued using my body for his pleasure, bending his knees and angling up to push in deeper and harder until all I could do was go limp in his grip and let the pleasure pulse through me as every inch of him stretched me open.

"*Fuck.*" With a snarl, he came, pumping a few more times to fill me as I stretched out my fingers, bracing myself.

Draven lowered my feet to the floor, and I took a moment to regain my senses, crouched on the carpet before turning awkwardly and getting up to face him.

He was smirking again, and I ran my fingers between my thighs, shuddering when I hit my sensitive clit. My pussy was slick with our cum. Draven dropped himself onto the couch, his cock still hard and glistening with my juices, bouncing with the movement. "Do you still want to talk?"

I smiled, removed my hand from between my legs, and fought the urge to cup my hands in front of myself, certain I'd be punished for trying to hide my nakedness from Draven. "Maybe."

He patted his thigh. "Take a seat."

I moved to sit on his lap, and he shook his head. "Not like that." Grabbing my thighs, he guided me to straddle him, and when I squirmed in his grip, he yanked me downward, penetrating me again and pulling me to sit. I moaned, opening my eyes to find him smirking at me.

"I thought we were going to talk."

"We are." Draven held my hips still, lifting his to thrust slowly in and out of me, making me whimper and shudder. "So talk."

"I... I think..."

"What's the matter, kitten?" He continued the slow drag of his thrusts, teasing me. "Can't think straight?"

Biting my lip, I couldn't pull my attention from the sensation of him fucking me. My clit still ached. Would the throbbing ever stop? Every orgasm only made me want more. I forced myself to concentrate. "I-I think I'm going to move to another town."

"Yeah?" He continued thrusting, and my eyes fluttered closed as I tried to concentrate on what I was saying and not the buildup of pleasure that rose in me with his every movement.

"Start new. Start afresh."

"That's good news, kitten."

I smiled before gasping as he thrust up hard into me. "But I need money."

"Sell the house."

"It's not mine to sell."

His eyebrow arched. "I'll make sure it is."

I bit my lip, placing my hands on his shoulders and riding him for a moment, debating if I wanted to know what he meant by that and how he was going to do it. Lolling my head back, I closed my eyes, smiling at the ceiling. Part of me wanted to know, but a bigger part didn't care. I didn't want more than my fair share. I'd sell the house and split the profits fifty-fifty with Owen—that didn't bother me. I had no intention of taking more than half.

All I wanted was the means to start my life over,

for a fresh start on everything he took away from me. *Was that too much to ask?*

This was the opportunity Draven gave me to be whoever I wanted to be.

As long as I stayed true to him.

Career-wise, did I want to stick with marketing? I think I did but maybe something more behind-the-scenes. Maybe advertisements and logo design. Maybe I could work from home. Then, at least I wouldn't need to worry about Draven showing up and fucking me over my desk.

Although the thought was enticing.

His voice penetrated my consciousness, interrupting my drifting thoughts. I cried out as he reached up, gripped my hair in his fist, and yanked my head back. "Come back to me, kitten." He nibbled at my ear. "Where did you go? Thinking of your future?" I tried nodding, but when I couldn't because of his grip on my hair, I answered, "Yes…"

"But there was something else you were thinking of right at the end there…"

"I was thinking about you appearing in my new office and fucking me over my desk."

He growled, the sound merging into a hum. "And you liked it."

It wasn't a question, but I jerked my head in a

shaky nod anyway.

Draven snarled and tilted his hips, pressing his feet flat against the floor and thrusting hard into me. "You can think about moving to another town soon, kitten," he said, his breathing coming in heavy pants as he fucked me harder. "But for the next week, you're staying right here, and I'm going to fuck you until you pass out from exhaustion." I gasped as he let my hair go and pulled me forward for a messy kiss as he probed my mouth with his tongue. When he released me, he dragged his teeth along my lower lip, whispering against my skin, "Maybe I'll let you rest for a few hours and wake you up with my tongue in your cunt."

"Yess…"

I wanted that.

I wanted it all.

I wanted a future where I could do what I desired.

I wanted a life where around every corner, Draven was waiting to fuck me hard in this life and the next.

He had my body and soul, and I smiled.

I didn't regret any of it.

CHAPTER 20

DRAVEN

Six Months Later

She couldn't see me, not yet, not until I wanted her to.

I couldn't help but watch her with pride, my Amelia.

Look how far she had come.

She'd moved from the house she'd shared with Owen within a month of summoning me, found a new job in a bigger city within two, and flourished. I swelled with pride at my kitten. She'd called me to her, not even knowing how much she needed me. This was about more than revenge, even if that was the spark that churned the fire in her to take action.

This was about claiming back everything she was. Everything she had lost over the years under the thumb of that excuse for a man, Owen. He'd broken her down as much as he could into the pliable housewife he wanted, and when she bent as far as she could but refused to break, he'd destroyed her.

And I'd given her everything back and more.

Amelia was moving around her office, her cell pressed to her ear as she discussed some work stuff with someone. I didn't care to find out more. I was simply enjoying the lines of her legs in the pencil skirt she was wearing.

Here's something Amelia didn't know I knew.

She had the opportunity to work from home full-time. She had a nice, large apartment with a home office, and all her work could be done remotely. But she'd *asked* if she could have an office in the building that she could use two days a week because she said it made her feel more like *part of the team.*

Chuckling darkly and hidden in the shadows, I watched her, and my cock was already hard at the sheer sight of her. *I* think she wanted an office because she couldn't get the idea out of her head of being *fucked* here, of being completely owned by me, where anyone could walk in and see her.

Well, here I was.

I'd seen her previous days, her gaze shooting up and darting around the room midway through some paperwork, as though she heard me and was hoping, *wishing* I would come out and claim her. It was more fun to make her wait, to keep her guessing until she was on the brink of thinking it wouldn't happen, and I only ever came to her in her new home. But I couldn't wait any longer, the game was growing thin for me, and it was time to claim my prize.

The sun cast bright rays through the floor-to-ceiling window behind her desk, the city a maze of toy cars and buildings full of people playing out their day on the streets below. We were only four stories up, but it was enough to give the illusion we were separated from the world, above it even.

How many people would see her bare ass pressed against the glass? Or her palms as she tried to find purchase against the window while her needy cunt took my cock from behind.

Glancing at her watch, Amelia sighed, a slight smile playing on her perfectly painted lips as she stood and stretched her arms over her head. As she left the office to make her midmorning coffee, I slipped under her desk, waiting for her to return.

The chair squeaked as she dropped into it, and she released another sigh of contentment as she sipped her coffee. Much too much sugar if you ask me. I'd previously tasted it on her lips and tongue, and she'd only chuckled when I complained about it.

Amelia's legs parted in front of me, and slowly I solidified, careful not to disturb the desk around me despite the cramped space. Her mound was on display, covered unfairly by black panties. Reaching out a finger, I wasn't able to slip my hand between her thighs without her feeling the brush of my skin on hers, and Amelia jolted, hitting her knees on the underside of the desk as I stroked a finger up her slit.

"Draven!" She gasped, her hands coming to grip the desk.

"Keep working. Amelia. You're busy."

"I..." She shuddered, stuttering through whatever it was she was going to say as I slipped her panties to the side and slid a finger inside her warmth, always waiting for me.

"Mmm..." I hummed, curling my finger inside her, "What a good girl... always wet for me."

When she started squirming, I grabbed her thighs and spread them, growling as I tongued at her sweet cunt. It was never enough for me. Every taste of her only fueled me on, and every time we parted, I thought of only when I'd get the next taste.

"Draven," Amelia panted, her hands coming down to grip at my hair. "Stop, please…"

She gasped as there was a knock on her office door, followed by the almost immediate sound of the door swinging open, sliding against the thick carpet.

I didn't stop.

"Amelia, glad I caught you."

I suppressed a growl at the man's voice. Who was this fucker who even *dared* to talk to my kitten? But Amelia's hand tightened its grip on my hair, trying to yank me away from her pussy as I continued to languidly lick her. Her other hand was poised on top of the desk, tapping a pen against paper. I didn't listen to whatever the intruder was saying but was enjoying immensely the way Amelia's thighs tightened around my head. Was she trying to hold me close or push me away? I don't think even she knew at this point. When I sunk two fingers inside her, she groaned, cutting off the sound and clearing her throat, ending in a fake cough. I chuckled quietly, pumping my fingers in her as she desperately tried to end the conversation with the intruder.

He finally stopped talking, and the door closed. When his footsteps had faded away, Amelia hissed at me. "That was my *boss*, Draven."

Between licks, I chuckled. "I don't know why you're telling me, kitten. I don't care." I sucked hard on her clit, and her hips bucked toward my face as she moaned, combing her fingers through my hair as it fell across her thighs. "We had a deal. I can take you whenever I want. Besides…" I looked up at her from under the desk, her eyes gazing lazily back at me, hooded and full of desire, "… I know you were simply waiting for this, *desperate* for the day I'd claim you in public."

She went to speak, and I ignored her attempts to argue, adding another finger inside her and focusing my tongue on her sensitive clit. "Don't even try to deny it, kitten. You know I can read you."

She clamped her mouth shut, biting down on her bottom lip. I thought she was going to argue again, but instead, she whispered, "Don't stop. Please."

I hummed with satisfaction as she clenched around my fingers and darted my tongue out over her clit, circling it before pursing my lips to suck hard on the bundle of nerves. Amelia was jerking against me now, the chair squeaking in protest until

I growled and held her still, pushing her pleasure over the edge until she bit her hand, muffling her cries as she came.

Amelia slumped in her chair, and I moved out from under her desk, unfolding myself and drawing to my full height, towering over her as she gazed up at me, still seated and clutching a palm to her chest. Her eyes widened when my lips curled into a smirk, and I slammed my palms on the arms of her chair, darting my tongue out to lick at her lips. Her eyes shot down to glance at my cock as it twitched in response to her attention.

"Do you ever wear clothes?" she whispered.

I cocked an eyebrow. "Why would I?"

Her teeth grazed her bottom lip as she pulled her gaze from mine, her cheeks flaming. "So I have something to take off of you for once."

"Ooh, my kinky little kitten. If that's what you want, it can be arranged." She smiled at me like I'd just granted all her birthday wishes at once, and I laughed. "But another time," I answered before spinning her chair and tipping it roughly, forcing her to stumble as she almost fell from it.

The chair hit the wall as I shoved it to the side, advancing on Amelia as she righted herself. When she was backed against the glass, her chest rising and falling against mine, and her excited heart rate thumped in my ears, I planted my hands on either side of her head and boxed her in.

"Turn around and bend over."

"Draven…"

She squeaked as I landed a sharp slap against her ass, and she glared at me. "Just because I like you, kitten, doesn't mean you get to talk back to me. When I give you a command, you obey."

Her lip quirked, and I'm certain she was holding back a smile, wondering what would happen if she continued to disobey me.

Also something we could explore another time.

Perhaps she didn't want her ass so red she couldn't sit comfortably halfway through her workday.

Not this time…

Amelia did as I asked, hitched up her tight skirt over her thighs and bent, presenting herself to me and crossing her arms against the window so she could rest her forehead. Pulling her panties to the side, I penetrated her, relishing in her gasp and quiet moans as she tried to keep herself quiet.

Picking up the pace of my thrusts, I gripped her hair and yanked her head back. "Look out the window, Amelia. Do you think anyone in the building across from you can see you?" She squealed as I pounded into her harder, pushing deep and pulling all the way out before doing it again. "What do you suppose they think you're doing? Stretching your back out, maybe?" I laughed as she moaned, squeezing her eyes shut and arching her back into my touch.

Pushing her roughly to her hands and knees, I kept her facing the window, and I continued to fuck her hard, groaning as I neared my peak. Amelia clenched deliciously around me with the change of angle, every thrust hitting that spot inside her that made her squirm when I used my fingers.

"I want you to come with me, kitten. I want you to come around my cock."

"Yess..."

Grabbing her upper arms, I pulled her toward me, forcing her back to arch as I pounded into her. "Come for me, Amelia... *now.*"

She shuddered and convulsed around my cock, milking my cum from me as her sweet cunt squeezed my dick. To stop from shouting out, I leaned forward and bit into her shoulder, slapping a palm over her mouth to cover her screams.

Amelia stayed on her knees, falling back to her hands as she panted, whimpering when I pulled from her. I used my fingers to push my cum back into her cunt before sliding her panties into place.

Standing, I chuckled as she turned to look over her shoulder at me. "Careful, kitten, you stay in that position, and I'm going to fuck you again." Amelia's lips parted, her eyes flashing with lust as I smirked. I held a hand out and helped Amelia to her feet, reaching out for support when her legs trembled before I lowered her into the chair. With my hands on the arms of the chair again, I leaned forward, brushing my lips over hers and loving the whimper she made as she tried to steal a kiss. "I'll see you at home tonight."

"Will you be staying for dinner?"

I watched her for a moment. She asked me to stay for dinner as often as she asked me to stay overnight, and I'd stopped saying no about two months ago. She treated me as more than a demon to fuck and draw pleasure from, as more than a bargain when her body and soul became mine. Quirking an eyebrow, I couldn't help but study her hazel eyes.

She was stronger but somehow still so innocent.

No wonder I couldn't resist the call of her soul to me. She was *made* to be owned by me.

"Yes, Amelia, I'll be there for dinner."

"And dessert?" she asked with a smirk.

I laughed. "You're such a good kitten. How did I get so lucky to find you?"

She lifted a shoulder, looking at her lap. "I called to you, and you answered."

My brows furrowed even as I smiled. She was more than I imagined, more than I felt worthy of, stirring sensations in my chest where there should be none. But we had a lifetime to figure it out, more than a lifetime, and she was always there for me when I came for her, waiting and willing. Sometimes after we fucked, she would comb her fingers through my hair, humming to herself, the gesture so innocent I had to fight the desire to pull away.

But I wouldn't pull away, and I wouldn't leave her.

Not *now*.

Not *ever*.

She was mine to worship as I was hers.

I licked her across the seam of her lips again and let her pull me in for a deep kiss when her hands darted out to grab my horns and yanked me closer, circling her fingers around the base the way I liked. Growling, I gripped the arms of the chair, the metal warping slightly before I pulled away.

"Naughty kitten, trying to get me worked up again. You'll pay for that later."

She smirked. The confident woman she was now peeking through after her previous shyness. "I'm counting on it."

Standing, I lowered her hands to her lap after unwrapping them from my horns. "I'll see you tonight. Don't keep me waiting."

Amelia smiled and turned back to her desk as I vanished from her sight, lingering to watch her from the shadows for a while.

I'd never get enough of her.

Worship me, kitten, and I'll worship you.

Your love gives me strength.

ACKNOWLEDGMENTS

Wow. Just wow.

I took a bit of a detour on my writing journey to bring some demon smut, and I don't think this book needs any further explanation than that. This is the first time I've ever had the cover before I started the book, but I was just so taken by it I had to have it, and all I could think of writing was some smutty fun, and why not?

Of course, it's not that simple. Once I implant an idea in my head, I need to let it fester for a few days before I put any words down. The story became dark in parts, and boy, do I love a character you love to hate.

And more so when that character gets what's coming to them.

So, I hope you enjoyed *Demonic*! I can't say for sure if there'll be others along this line. I'm sorry, I wish I could. Maybe I'll make a mini-series, and I'll add it to the already extensive list of books I have planned to write! Or maybe this one will simply live on its own little pedestal.

CONNECT WITH ME ONLINE

ANGELS AND FIRE BOOKS
Find our exciting stories at:
www.angelsandfirebooks.com.au

READER GROUP

Want access to fun, prizes and sneak peeks?
Join my Facebook Reader Group.
https://www.facebook.com/groups/588038442170571

Demonic

NEWSLETTER

Sign up for my Newsletter.
https://www.subscribepage.com/angelsandfirebooks

BOOKBUB

https://www.bookbub.com/authors/stefanie-dawn

GOODREADS

Add my books to your TBR list
on my Goodreads profile.
https://www.goodreads.com/author/
show/21761217.Stefanie_Dawn

AMAZON

https://www.amazon.com/author/stefaniedawn

WEBSITE

http://www.angelsandfirebooks.com.au/

INSTAGRAM

https://www.instagram.com/angelsandfirebooks

EMAIL

info@angelsandfirebooks.com.au

FACEBOOK

https://www.facebook.com/stefaniedawnwriter

ABOUT THE AUTHOR

Stefanie Dawn has been a writer and creative soul all her life **and** strives to give her readers stories they can escape into as they become absorbed in the worlds created.

When she isn't writing, Stefanie might be painting, reading, or watching movies. She loves the process of producing films as another form of storytelling. There's also a good chance she'll be baking some delicious treats—pretending she won't later regret consuming them—or simply enjoying a cocktail with friends.

Stefanie Dawn lives in South Australia with her ever-supportive partner and a lovable gang of rescue cats.

You can stay up to date with
Stefanie and her books at:
www.angelsandfirebooks.com.au

www.ingramcontent.com/pod-product-compliance
Lightning Source LLC
Chambersburg PA
CBHW030945210726
48290CB00007B/2326